TO ESTHER AND ROSIE

HOPE JONES
WILL <u>NOT</u> EAT MEAT

JOSH LACEY

ILLUSTRATED BY
BEATRIZ CASTRO

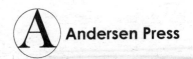

BE KIND.
BE VEGAN.

First published in 2021 by
Andersen Press Limited
20 Vauxhall Bridge Road
London SW1V 2SA

www.andersenpress.co.uk

2 4 6 8 10 9 7 5 3 1

British Library Cataloguing in Publication Data available.

ISBN 978 1 78344 939 2

This book is printed on FSC accredited paper

Printed and bound in Great Britain by Clays Ltd, Elcograf S.p.A.

I'M GIVING UP
MEAT TO
SAVE OUR
WORLD!

I'M NOT GOING
TO STOP TILL I
CHANGE THE
WORLD!

❧ Hope Jones' Blog ❧

Hello.
Welcome to my blog.

My name is Hope Jones.
I am ten years old.
I am going to save the world.

'Wilderness is not a luxury but a necessity of the human spirit, and as vital to our lives as water and good bread'

Edward Abbey

'We are, quite literally, gambling with the future of our planet – for the sake of hamburgers'

PETER SINGER

'YOU ARE NEVER TOO SMALL TO MAKE A DIFFERENCE'

GRETA THUNBERG

'Wilbur burst into tears. "I don't want to die," he moaned. "I want to stay alive, right here in my comfortable manure pile with all my friends. I want to breathe the beautiful air and lie in the beautiful sun."'

CHARLOTTE'S WEB, E B White

'IN OUR WORLD, EVERYBODY THINKS OF CHANGING HUMANITY, AND NOBODY THINKS OF CHANGING HIMSELF'

LEO TOLSTOY

'There is no fundamental difference between man and animals in their ability to feel pleasure and pain, happiness, and misery'

CHARLES DARWIN

'Big impact change starts with the individual. No one else can bring what you have. You show up, you say yes, and then you bring your magic'

Kelsey Juliana

Hope Jones' Blog

SATURDAY 1 MARCH

Hello!

I have to tell you some very exciting news. I am a vegetarian.

It happened like this . . . After breakfast, Mum and I walked to the shops. It was just us two, because Dad had taken my little brother Finn to football practice, and my big sister Becca was still in bed.

We're boycotting supermarkets, because they use so much plastic. Instead we buy everything from our local shops. Walking around them takes a bit longer than pushing a trolley up and down the aisles or ordering stuff online, but we get a chance to chat to everyone. I've become good friends with our local shopkeepers. Like Katya, the baker, who often gives us a free doughnut or an extra slice of poppy seed cake.

I always like chatting with Mr Zaimoglu in Bosphorus. He sells fresh vegetables, unusual fruits, and hundreds of different spices, and can tell you something interesting about all of them. Like: do you know the difference between a Medjool and a Deglet Noor? Do you even know what they are? (I didn't, but I do now: they're both types of dates. And they're both delicious!)

Mitch the butcher makes me laugh. He's the local joker. Mitch always has a sign outside his shop and, at least once a week, he writes a different slogan on the board. Sometimes it's funny, sometimes it's serious, and sometimes it's a special offer.

Today the sign wasn't the only thing outside Mitch's shop. Sparkle was there too. I love Sparkle, she is one of my favourite people in the whole world. I got to know her when I started protesting against plastic. She comes round to our house quite often, because she is good friends with Becca's boyfriend Tariq.

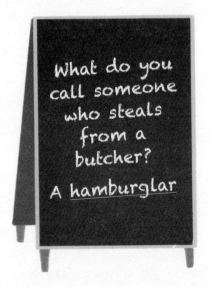

What do you call someone who steals from a butcher?

A hamburglar

I was very surprised to see her outside Mitch's shop. I said, 'What are you doing here?'

'I'm holding a protest,' she said. 'Like yours.'

I couldn't understand why Sparkle was protesting. I didn't know there was anything wrong with meat.

Sparkle said, 'What is meat?'

'Animals,' I said.

'Dead animals,' Sparkle said. 'Your roast chicken. Your bacon sandwich. Your burger. They were all animals once. Living, breathing animals, just like you or me. Then they were killed, simply to satisfy the hunger of a human. Don't you think that's wrong?'

I don't like the idea of eating a dead animal, but I've always done it. And meat is quite delicious.

'I don't want an animal to die for my dinner,' Sparkle said. 'But that's not the only thing wrong with eating meat. The meat industry is a major cause of climate change.'

I was very surprised to hear that.

Sparkle said, 'Didn't you read my book?'

'Which book?' I said.

'The book I gave you.'

To be honest, I had completely forgotten about that book. Sparkle gave it to me a couple of months ago. I was very busy at the time, protesting against plastic, so I put the book on my shelf and never took it out again.

'You should read it,' Sparkle said.

'I will,' I promised. 'As soon as I get home.'

'For now,' Sparkle said, 'you can read this.' She gave me a leaflet.

6

STOP AND THINK

BEFORE YOU SHOP!

BEFORE YOU BUY MEAT FROM THIS BUTCHER, PLEASE THINK ABOUT YOUR CHOICES

There are many good reasons to stop eating meat.

1. Eating meat is wrong. Why should a chicken perish for your lunch? Why should a sheep suffer for your supper? Why should any animals have to die simply so you can have a nice meal?

2. Eating meat causes climate change. Livestock farming produces approximately a fifth of our greenhouse gas emissions. Which is more than the emissions from ships, planes, trucks, cars and all other transport added together.

3. Eating meat is unfair. Right now, some of us eat meat while others starve. We could easily feed all the people on this planet if everyone switched to a vegan diet.

4. Eating meat is making us sick. Eating meat is linked to heart disease, diabetes and cancer.

Be Kind. Be Vegan.

Follow me for more information
@sparklethevegan #sparklethevegan

Sparkle told me all about her protest. She is going to demonstrate outside Mitch's shop every weekend until he stops selling the flesh of dead animals.

'What does Mitch think about that?' I asked her.

'I haven't asked him,' Sparkle admitted.

She would like to do her protest every day, not just Saturdays, but she has to go to school during the week.

As soon as I got home, I started reading Sparkle's book and learning a lot more about being a vegetarian. It was amazing. Sparkle is absolutely right – the meat industry is a major cause of climate change, because of the farts. You might think I'm joking, but I'm not – farting cows cause global warming.

It's not just cows. It's pigs, chickens and sheep too. Their farts are made of methane, which goes into the atmosphere and causes global warming.

Their poo is bad for the environment too. So is the water that they drink, and the food that they eat, and the lorries that carry them around, and all the other pollution and emissions connected to the meat industry.

After reading Sparkle's book, I know that there is one very simple way to save the world: stop eating meat! So I'm now a vegetarian. I haven't eaten any meat all day.

Hope Jones' Blog

SUNDAY 2 MARCH

What's your favourite food? Mine is lasagna. I love lasagna . . . juicy, tomatoey, cheesy lasagna. Mmmmmmm. I love it.

Being a vegetarian is mostly very easy. This morning, I had porridge for breakfast. There aren't any animals in oats. The problems started at lunchtime. Because: lasagna. Dad apologised again and again. He had completely forgotten that I am now a vegetarian. Next time he'll make a special veggie lasagna just for me.

I don't mind. I'm having beans on toast instead, it's not as nice as lasagna, but I'll be fine.

I have been a vegetarian for two whole days. I can't have saved a pig yet, or a cow, but I have saved a bit of each. I didn't have the lasagna for lunch. Or ham sandwiches for tea, I had cheese instead.

Obviously I'm not going to save the world on my own, I'm just one person, but at least I'm making a difference.

I talked to Mr Crabbe who lives next door. I asked him if he had ever considered becoming a vegetarian. He said he doesn't like vegetables, which I must admit is a bit of a problem.

I asked Dad if he would consider becoming a vegetarian.

'Definitely,' he said. 'As long as I can carry on eating steak, burgers, sausages, and bacon sandwiches.'

I wish he could be serious sometimes.

I asked Mum if she might become a vegetarian. She said, 'Maybe. We'll see. I'll think about it when I'm not so busy.' When she talks like that, she usually means no.

I asked Finn. He said, 'Not in a million years,' which obviously means no too.

Becca was the only person who said yes, because she is already a part-time vegetarian. I didn't even know that. She never eats meat when she and Tariq are together. From today, she's going to try and be vegetarian at home too. I am very proud of her. Thank you, Becca! Thank you, Tariq!

There is only one member of our family who definitely won't become vegetarian: our cat, Poppadom.

I have been doing some research on the internet and apparently cats have to eat meat. That's what vets say.

I also read about the ingredients of cat food and it is really quite disgusting.

Cat food is all the yucky bits of animals that people won't eat. Their feet, for instance. And their guts, brains, ears, whiskers, nostrils, and all the other sticky, slimy bits that can't be made into anything else.

I really don't like thinking about it. All those brains and guts and slimy bits stuffed into a tin, which is sitting on a shelf in our fridge. Gross.

Luckily hamsters don't eat meat.

Poppadom can't become a vegetarian, that's just the way she is. Some things can't change, but some things can. And some people too.

Hope Jones' Blog

MONDAY 3 MARCH

I usually love school burgers. They're so tasty!

Unfortunately they're stuffed with beef. Which is why I had this for my lunch:

Apparently it's a mushroom burger, although it didn't taste anything like a burger or a mushroom. In fact, it tasted of nothing.

Luckily it came with chips or I would have gone hungry. Which would have been a big problem, because we have PE on Monday afternoons, and PE is not much fun on an empty stomach.

I hope the vegetarian school lunches aren't always like this, or being a vegetarian is going to be more difficult than I had expected.

Jemima Higginbotham said, 'If you don't like the veggie option, there's a very simple solution.'

DURDLE PRIMARY
Lunch Menu
Monday 3rd March

MAIN
Beef burger

VEGETARIAN OPTION
Mushroom burger

VEGETABLES
Chips and salad

DESSERT
Banana custard

I said, 'What's that?'

She said, 'Eat the meat. It's so tasty! I love burgers. Mmmmm.'

My friend Harry thinks I am wasting my time, worrying about meat so much. He says I should just eat what I want, because very soon scientists will invent a food product which is entirely carbon neutral.

'All our nutritional needs will be satisfied by a few pills,' Harry said. 'You won't need to eat anything else. We won't need animals, or farms. We won't even need food. You'll just take a pill in the morning and that will fill you up for the whole day.'

Harry thinks science is going to solve all our problems.

'You just have to wait a few years till I'm a bit older,' he said. 'I'll invent some foods which don't cause climate change.'

'What if the planet has been destroyed before you've had a chance to grow up?' I said.

Harry didn't know the answer to that, unfortunately.

I don't know what to think about Harry's ideas. I hope he's right, because it would be wonderful if we could survive on pills which don't emit any carbon or cause climate change. But I can't help hoping we find a different solution, because I would miss real food so much. Imagine never having chips again, or ice cream, or chocolate eclairs, or waffles drenched in maple syrup, or a gummy bear.

That would be so sad.

TUESDAY 4 MARCH

We need to talk about farts, because I am confused.

At lunch, Harry asked me a question. He said, 'What are your farts made of?'

'Methane,' I said.

Methane is why farts smell so bad.

Harry said, 'Do you know what a cow's farts are made of?'

'Methane,' I said.

Harry said, 'So your farts are made of the same thing as a cow's farts?'

'I suppose so.'

'Then why are a cow's farts so terrible for the planet, but your farts are fine?'

I did not know the answer to that.

Harry said, 'If you want to save the world and stop global warming, shouldn't you stop farting too? Shouldn't you stop eating so many lentils and beans? They make you fart a lot, don't they? If eating a cow is bad, isn't eating beans just as bad? Or even worse?'

They were all very good questions. I felt embarrassed because I didn't know any of the answers.

Harry wasn't trying to embarrass me, he would never do anything like that, he's my best friend. But he does ask questions that make my head hurt.

Sometimes Miss Brockenhurst sighs when Harry puts up

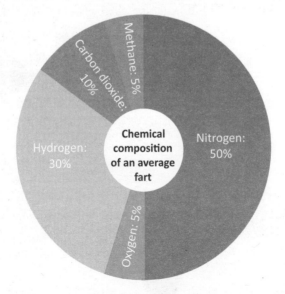

his hand, because she knows he is going to ask her a difficult question. Today it was my turn to sigh, but he did ask me a very good question. If a cow's farts are killing the planet, aren't my farts killing the planet too?

When I got home, I tried to find the answer in Sparkle's book, and I looked on the internet, but I could find anything. So I asked Dad. 'Harry's right,' Dad said, 'you're killing the planet. I am too. You know the best way to stop climate change? Get rid of humans. We're the problem.'

I don't want to get rid of us. Dad doesn't either, but he's like Harry. He enjoys asking me difficult questions. I just wish I knew the answers.

Harry is obviously still thinking about farts too – he sent me this pie chart in an email. The subject line was, 'An average fart':

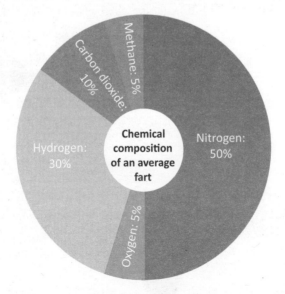

WEDNESDAY 5 MARCH

Today my lunch was cheese salad.

After I had scraped my plate, I talked to the dinner ladies, Mrs Darlington and Mrs Baptist, and asked if they could make the vegetarian option a bit nicer. They weren't very pleased about me asking that.

'We do our best,' Mrs Baptist said. 'Cooking for a whole school isn't easy, especially on our budget.'

Mrs Darlington said, 'How exactly would you like the lunches to be improved?'

I did have one suggestion for the vegetarian option: 'Maybe sometimes it could actually taste of something?'

Mrs Darlington said, 'Someone needs to teach you some manners, young lady.'

'We don't ask for thanks,' Mrs Baptist said. 'But a little politeness would be nice.'

I didn't mean to be rude. I know the dinner ladies have a difficult job, but I just wish the veggie lunches weren't always so brown and boring.

Harry has done some more research about cows. He has now discovered that the big problem isn't their farts. It's their burps.

Cow burps contain twenty times as much methane as cow farts. That's why cows are so bad for the environment: they burp too much!

Because humans are so much smaller than cows, and we only have one stomach, instead of four, our burps and farts don't emit very much methane into the atmosphere.

'You don't have to worry,' Harry said. 'You can carry on farting and burping as much as you like.' Which was a great relief.

Burp!

THURSDAY 6 MARCH

I have been reading the most vegetarian book in history: *Charlotte's Web.*

Have you read it? If not, you should. I won't tell you what happens in case you don't know the story already. But I will tell you this: I cannot imagine how anyone could read about Wilbur and ever want to eat sausages or bacon again.

FRIDAY 7 MARCH

Today I had a big row with Mrs Darlington and Mrs Baptist. I didn't want to, I didn't mean to, but it just happened. Because of the pasty.

> # DURDLE PRIMARY
> ## Lunch Menu
> ### Friday 7th March
>
> ### MAIN
> Fish fingers
>
> ### VEGETARIAN OPTION
> Cheese and leek pasty
>
> ### VEGETABLES
> Chips and oven-baked courgettes
>
> ### DESSERT
> Peach crumble with custard

I only ate one bite of the pasty, then I had to spit it out or I would have been sick. I didn't even try one bite of oven-baked courgettes because they looked so disgusting. Luckily the chips were nice.

Mrs Darlington saw I hadn't eaten much. She asked what was wrong. She said, 'Don't you like the pasty?'

Maybe I should have lied. Maybe I should have said I wasn't hungry. Maybe that would have been better.

But I told the truth. 'It's horrible,' I said. 'I can't eat it, I'll be sick.'

Mrs Darlington looked very upset. She actually looked as if she was going to cry. She rushed back into the kitchen and closed the door after her. Later I saw Mrs Baptist giving her a hug.

Miss Brockenhurst had words with me. (She's our teacher.)

Mr Khan did too. (He's the head.)

In break, I made a card to say sorry to Mrs Darlington and Mrs Baptist. I feel bad, I didn't mean to be rude to them. I just wish they could make nicer lunches for us vegetarians.

Dear Mrs Darlington and
Mrs Baptist
I am very sorry
for being rude.
Yours sincerely,
Hope Jones (Otters)

Sparkle says I did the right thing. She says you have to stick to your principles, even if that means upsetting people, because you're never going to change the world by being polite.

Sparkle finishes school early on Fridays, so she went protesting this afternoon. Becca and Tariq joined in.

Sparkle was very impressed that I have been a vegetarian for almost one whole week. She asked if I had made any of the recipes from her book.

'Not yet,' I had to admit. 'Maybe on Monday.'

'The Vegan Wellington is brilliant,' Sparkle said. 'It has beetroot and tofu instead of beef. Mmmmm! Just talking about it is making me hungry.'

Dad and I are going to try some of the recipes next week.

It will be good experience for me. That's what Dad says, anyway. Also I think he's looking forward to having some time off from cooking.

'It's so great that you're a vegetarian,' Sparkle said. 'Now you just have to take the next step and become a vegan.'

I couldn't actually remember the difference. Luckily she had another leaflet which explained it very clearly.

DINNER DOESN'T HAVE TO MEAN
D E A T H!

THINK BEFORE YOU EAT! WHO ARE YOU? WHO DO YOU WANT TO BE? THE CHOICE IS YOURS.

- Do you want to be a vegan? Vegans do not consume any animal products. Vegans don't eat meat or fish. Many vegans choose not to wear leather or wool.

- Do you want to be a vegetarian? Vegetarians do not eat meat. However, most vegetarians do consume animal products. Most vegetarians drink milk, and eat cheese, eggs and honey, and wear leather and wool. Animals have suffered to provide this food and clothing.

- If you don't choose to be a vegan or a vegetarian, then you have chosen to be one of these:

- A pescatarian: you eat fish.

- A carnivore: you eat meat.

- An omnivore: you eat everything and anything, living and dead.

We all have choices. We can be who we want to be.

Be Kind. Be Vegan.

Follow me for more information
@sparklethevegan #sparklethevegan

Sparkle pointed out that becoming vegetarian is pretty much pointless, because didn't I know where eggs and milk come from? And didn't I know how cows and chickens were treated?

I didn't, but I do now.

It's totally gross.

Becca thought so too. She would like to become a vegan, but she was worried about one thing: 'Will my hair fall out?' she said.

Sparkle laughed. 'No! Why would it?'

'I read an article which said so,' Becca said. 'It said vegans don't get enough nutrients so their hair falls out.'

'That's fake news,' Sparkle said. 'Look at my hair, is it falling out?'

'Vegans get more than enough vitamins and protein,' Sparkle explained. 'You just have to be careful about what you eat.'

While Becca and Sparkle were talking about their hair, Tariq told me more about factory farming. OMG. I still feel sick. Have you seen what they do to chickens in factory farms? And pigs? It is so gross! And really sad. Looking at those miserable animals made me want to cry.

Do you know what happens to a hen who lives on a factory farm? It spends its entire life in a cage which is the same size as a piece of paper. All day. All night. In that cage. From the day it is born to the day it dies. It never sees the sun, it never goes outside, it can hardly even turn around. It just eats and sleeps and lays eggs.

The protest was brilliant. Lots of people talked to us and took Sparkle's leaflets. I don't know how many of them will actually become vegans or vegetarians, but we've certainly made them think about what they eat.

Sparkle and I have made an arrangement to meet outside Mitch's again tomorrow morning and do another protest.

SATURDAY 8 MARCH

I've been a vegetarian for a whole week. It's been easy. In fact, it's been so easy, I'm going to stop being vegetarian, and become a vegan instead.

I am not going to consume any animal products. I will not eat meat, milk, cheese, eggs or honey. I will not wear leather or wool.

Mum has promised to buy oat milk for my breakfast. She hasn't had a chance yet, so I didn't eat any cereal today. Instead I had Dad's Full English.

Yum.

I had everything except the bacon and the eggs. It was still delicious. Dad makes the best breakfasts in the world.

Becca had the same as me. She's vegan too now. I just wish we could persuade the rest of our family to become vegans, or at least vegetarians. They could still eat cheese and eggs, but giving up meat would make a big difference to our planet.

Dad actually agrees with me. He wants to stop climate change, he hates factory farming, he wishes he could stop eating animals.

'You could,' I said, 'easily.'

'I know,' Dad said, 'but I just can't help myself.' Then he popped another crispy crunchy piece of bacon in his mouth.

After breakfast, Dad and Finn drove to football practice.

Becca went back to bed, because she's going to a party with Tariq tonight, so she needs her beauty sleep.

Mum and I walked to the shops. Mitch has a new sign.

I love vegetarians.

They taste fabulous roasted with garlic and rosemary

I texted Sparkle and asked why she wasn't protesting outside Mitch's shop. She texted back to say she was still in bed. Teenagers! She said, could I do the protest for her instead? Unfortunately I didn't have a banner or any leaflets, so I couldn't.

Mitch was very disappointed to hear that I have become a vegan. 'You're one of my best customers,' he said. 'I don't know what I'll do without you.'

I said I was sorry. I used to love eating meat, but the problem is: I want to save the world. And eating meat is killing the planet.

Mitch said he cares about the planet too, but he has to earn a living. So what is he supposed to do?

'You could stop eating meat,' I said.

'I'm a butcher,' Mitch said. 'How can I stop eating meat?

I couldn't sell meat to my customers if I'm not going to eat it myself.'

'You could sell vegetables instead,' I suggested.

'Then I wouldn't be a butcher,' Mitch said. 'Do you want me to close my shop? Do you want me to lose my job?'

Obviously I don't.

'I hate factory farming,' Mitch said. 'I hate cruelty to animals, but I can't see anything wrong with eating them if they live a comfortable and happy life first. I wouldn't mind being a sheep! Spending your days on a lovely green Welsh hillside, eating as much grass as you want. Once a year, you get your coat cut off and made into a jumper. What could be better?'

Mitch knows the farmers who breed the animals and supply his shop. He made the farmers sound really nice. He has pictures of them on his walls and goes to see them sometimes to meet the cows, the pigs, the sheep and the chickens. He says they care about their animals and they care about the planet too.

'I agree with you about one thing: people should eat less meat,' Mitch said. 'They should eat *better* meat. The meat I sell is more expensive than meat in a supermarket, because it's not mass-produced, it's not factory-farmed. The animals are treated decently and humanely – they have a good life, but that costs more. Unfortunately, most people just want the cheap stuff, they don't care where it comes from.'

Is Mitch right about different types of farming? Surely it's better to give up eating animals and animal products altogether. I want to save the planet and stop climate change. But I started feeling bad about my protest. I don't want Mitch to lose his job or his home. What am I supposed to do?

I texted Sparkle to ask her these questions, but she hasn't replied yet. I'll let you know as soon as she does.

When we were leaving, Mitch tried to tempt me with a sausage roll. He asked if I would like a free one. He knows how much I used to love them.

'Go on,' Mitch said. 'Take it. I'll be offended if you don't.'

I didn't really want his sausage roll. I was never going to eat it, but I took it anyway because I knew someone who would.

SUNDAY 9 MARCH

I'm feeling a bit depressed today because of Grandad. Don't worry! He hasn't died or anything. I had a big row with him, that's all, and I'm still feeling terrible about it. I love Grandad. I hate arguing with him. I didn't even want to have a row, but he was teasing me so much, I couldn't help myself.

Mum says he was the same when she was a girl, if not even worse, and I shouldn't mind because it's the only way he knows how to show affection.

Today we went to Granny and Grandad's house for Sunday lunch. Granny had made roast beef, which has always been my favourite lunch. I love the Yorkshire puddings, I love the potatoes, I love the gravy. Best of all, I love the beef. Especially made by Granny. Her roast beef is soooooo tasty.

Obviously I didn't eat any.

I didn't even have the gravy, because it's made from the meat. Instead I just ate potatoes, cabbage, carrots and two Yorkshire puddings. I had just finished one of them when Becca said, 'Don't you know what Yorkshire puddings are made of?'

Actually, I didn't.

'Flour, milk and eggs,' Granny said.

'Not very vegan,' Becca said. She was just eating the veg.

'A bit of milk won't hurt anyone,' Mum said. 'Let her enjoy her lunch.'

But I wanted to stick to my principles, so I gave my other

Yorkshire pudding to Finn, and I just had potatoes, cabbage and carrots. They were delicious. Granny is the best cook in the world. I didn't even mind not having any beef, gravy, or Yorkshire pudding.

What I did mind was Grandad teasing me and Becca about being vegan. He would not stop. He dangled a bit of beef in front of our faces and said, 'Doesn't that smell delicious?'

'Yes,' I said. I didn't want to lie. 'But I don't want any, thanks.'

'Have a taste,' Grandad said. 'Just an incy-wincy tiny taste.'

'No, thank you.'

'We're vegans,' Becca said, 'because we care about our planet and the future more than we care about our own pleasure.'

Grandad said, 'Don't you like your grandmother's cooking? Do you think she's a terrible cook? Is that what you're saying?'

'We love her cooking,' Becca said.

'We just don't want to eat animals,' I said.

'Eating meat is natural,' Grandad said. 'Humans have been doing it for thousands of years. I don't see why we should stop now.'

I said, 'Because of climate change.'

Grandad said, 'Not that again!'

Grandad doesn't believe in climate change. He says it's just made up by politicians and we shouldn't believe them. The world has always changed temperature and humans have nothing to do with it.

'I'll eat beef if I want to,' Grandad said. 'I don't want those do-gooders sticking their noses into my affairs. It's not their business what I eat.'

I started explaining about the meat industry and pollution and carbon emissions when he interrupted me.

'I don't care,' he said. 'I like beef, so I'll eat it. My house, my choice.'

Usually I don't take much notice of Grandad and his teasing and arguing. When he starts going on about politicians and the news and how everything used to be better in the old days, I move to the other end of the table and chat to Granny instead. But today I couldn't. Today was different.

I said, 'This is our planet. We're going to live here for the rest of our lives. Do you want to ruin it for us? What about our children? And our grandchildren? Climate change is going to mess up the planet for them. We have to change the way that we live – and that means changing what we eat.'

'What if climate change doesn't exist?' Grandad said.

'What if it does?' I said. 'What if it messes up the lives of your children, and your grandchildren, and your great-grandchildren? Don't you care about them?'

'I do,' Grandad admitted, 'but I don't see how me eating beef is going to make any difference.'

I started explaining about emissions again, but he wasn't listening.

He said, 'The world's gone mad. I don't know why we can't go back to how things used to be. When I was your age, boys were boys, and girls were girls, and there was none of this nonsense. No one talked about climate change. We just ate what we wanted. Good honest food. If it was good enough for me, I don't see why it's not good enough for you. Eating meat is just normal. It's natural. It's what humans do.'

'Humans used to kill their own meat,' I said. 'They used to hunt wild animals. That's very different to eating a factory-farmed chicken.'

'I would have been happy to kill this cow,' said Grandad.

'Me too,' said Finn.

'Liar,' I said. 'You wouldn't.'

'We would,' they both said.

Finn and Grandad got very excited about the idea of hunting animals together. They picked up their knives, and ran around the table, pretending to kill a cow.

Now they want to go and shoot a stag. Or some rabbits. Or pigeons.

I can't understand why anyone would want to do that for fun. What's so good about killing animals? I think it's horrible.

Everyone calmed down when Granny brought in the treacle tart and ice cream.

'None of that for the girls,' Grandad said. 'They don't eat milk, remember?'

'They can eat this,' Granny said.

Especially for us, she had made vegan treacle tart and bought a tub of vegan vanilla ice cream. It was just as nice as normal ice cream. Everyone said so, even Grandad.

I don't really care about Grandad teasing me. He's a teaser, that's who he is. He can't help himself.

Also, he is extremely old. Things were different when he was growing up. His ideas are stuck in the past.

I just wish he could understand about climate change. It might not ruin his life, because he probably won't be here any more. But it's going to ruin ours.

MONDAY 10 MARCH

I have some exciting news. I'm going to be on the school council.
I will be, anyway, if enough people vote for me.

Durdle Primary
We love learning!
This term's values are persistence and resilience.

School Council Elections

This term you have the opportunity to vote for
your class representative on the school council.
Each class will elect one representative.
Anyone can put themselves forward as a candidate.
The election will be held on **Friday 21st March**.
If you wish to apply, please complete this form and
hand it to your teacher by **Thursday 13th March**.

- -

School Council Elections Application

NAME: Hope Jones

CLASS: Otters

WHY I WANT TO BE ON THE SCHOOL COUNCIL:
To save the world

I know one other person who wants to be on the school council – Jemima Higginbotham. I hope no one votes for her. She is so bossy! I couldn't bear it if she was elected and I wasn't.

One person has been inspired by my campaign: Finn is standing for the school council for his own class. But he's not going to campaign about changing the menus or anything to do with climate change. Instead, he wants to turn the school into a water park. The playground will be an enormous pool and the teachers can teach us how to do the rides.

'That is the silliest idea I've ever heard,' I told him.

'I think it would be fun,' Finn said.

He hasn't started writing his speech yet, but he has drawn a picture of the big slide that will come down from the school's roof if he wins.

Hope Jones' Blog

TUESDAY 11 MARCH

I have made my first ever vegan meal.

Usually Dad does the cooking, and sometimes Mum, but today was my turn. I made chickpea fritters with a smoky aubergine dip dotted with pomegranate seeds and flavoured with tahini. It looked delicious in the picture in the recipe book, but it didn't look quite so nice in real life.

The chickpea fritters might not have looked perfect, but they tasted great. I thought so, anyway. So did Becca and Mum. They both loved them.

'This is fabulous,' Dad said. 'Can I have seconds, please?' He hadn't even finished his firsts. I knew he was just being nice, but I didn't mind.

Only one person wasn't so happy. Finn pushed his plate away and said, 'I'm not hungry.'

'You must be starving,' Mum said. 'You've been at school all day. Just try it.'

'I have tried it,' Finn said. 'That's how I know I don't like it.'

I reminded him that you don't have to eat meat at every meal.

'I don't mind not eating meat,' Finn said. 'I just don't like this.'

In the end, he had cheese on toast.

WEDNESDAY 12 MARCH

I'm feeling sick. Because of the pig.

Don't worry! I haven't eaten one, I'm still a veggie. I'm feeling sick because I saw what happens to pigs in factory farms.

I wanted to educate Finn, so I said to him, 'Do you want to watch a movie?'

He said, 'Sure.'

We watched a film about factory farming. It's easy to find on the internet, but I wouldn't recommend watching it yourself, because it is unbelievably disgusting.

We had only watched three minutes when Finn said he was going to vomit.

I felt like vomiting too. I would have preferred to switch off the movie, but I knew I had to keep watching. I need all the information at my fingertips, so I can discuss the issues with people and convince them of my arguments. When Mum came in and saw what we were watching, she made me turn it off. She doesn't want Finn to have nightmares, or me either.

'What about the pigs?' I said. 'They must be having nightmares, stuck in that factory all day and all night. Don't you care about them?'

'I care about you more,' Mum said.

I had a question for Finn. 'Now you know what happens in factory farms, are you going to stop eating meat?'

He's not sure. He doesn't want pigs to suffer like that, or any other animals. 'The thing is,' he said, 'I love eating meat.'

'Vegetarian meals can be delicious too,' I pointed out.

'But I want to be a footballer,' Finn said. 'You can't be fast and strong if you don't eat meat.'

'Of course you can,' I said.

'You can't,' Finn said.

'There are lots of vegetarian athletes,' I said.

'No, there aren't,' Finn said. He was absolutely sure about it.

I'm going to prove him wrong.

FROM Hope Jones
TO Marcus Wilton
DATE Wednesday 12 March
SUBJECT Meat and my brother

Dear Mr Wilton

Please can you help me?

My brother Finn is obsessed with football. You are his favourite player – he thinks you're brilliant. He says you are the best young footballer in the world and you're definitely going to win the Golden Boot at the next World Cup, or maybe the one after.

He has a poster of you on his wall. He watches your videos every day. His ambition is scoring a goal as good as the one you scored against Crystal Palace.

But he doesn't believe you're a vegetarian.

I have recently stopped eating meat, because I am worried about climate change. I would like my family to stop too. But Finn refuses to become a vegetarian, because he thinks he needs meat to make him big and strong enough to be a professional footballer.

Could you please tell him he's wrong?

Thank you!

Yours sincerely

Hope Jones

THURSDAY 13 MARCH

Today Miss Brockenhurst announced the names of the candidates for the school council elections.

There are only three: me, Jemima and Vivek.

We each had to stand up and say a few words about ourselves.

1: Jemima Higginbotham

Jemima has a lot of ideas for the school council. If she is elected to the school council, she is going to ban homework. She wants each class to get their own pet, and the children will take the pets home at the weekends. Also she wants to change the school policy on wet play, so everyone can go to the art room.

They're actually really good ideas, especially about the class pet. If she wins, I hope we get a puppy.

2: Vivek Sidhu

I don't know why Vivek wants to be on the school council. He doesn't seem to know either. His manifesto is ridiculous. He says we should get rid of lessons and just play sport instead: football in the winter; cricket in the summer. All day long.

I asked what would be the point of that, and he said, 'It's better than maths and English.'

Actually he's wrong. Maths and English are both useful, whereas football and cricket aren't.

Vivek said football and cricket are useful if you want to be a footballer or a cricketer. But I don't.

3: Hope Jones

Obviously that's me. If I am elected to the school council, I am going to save the world. And make our school dinners a bit nicer.

Durdle Primary
We love learning!

This term's values are persistence and resilience.

School Council Elections

Three students have proposed themselves as your representative on the school council. They are your three candidates. You must choose between them and decide who will get your vote.

Your three candidates are:

Jemima Higginbotham

Vivek Sidhu

Hope Jones

The election will be held on **Friday 21st March**. Before the vote, the three candidates will present their ideas to the class and you will have an opportunity to ask questions.

You will only be able to vote for ONE candidate. Please think carefully before making your decision.

There are thirty kids in our class. At break, I asked everyone who they are intending to vote for. Most of them wouldn't tell me: some said they hadn't decided yet, others said it was a secret.

I don't believe anyone will vote for Vivek. Except himself, obviously, and maybe some of the kids who love sports. Which means I probably need fifteen people to vote for me if I'm going to win the election.

Harry promised he will vote for me. He's my best friend. I would be shocked if he didn't. Selma says she will too. Plus I'll vote for myself, which makes three. So I only need twelve more votes.

Jemima has seven best friends, plus her makes eight. Eight votes for her and three for me. Plus one for Vivek. Which leaves eighteen kids who haven't yet made up their minds. Somehow I have to persuade twelve of those eighteen kids to vote for me rather than Jemima.

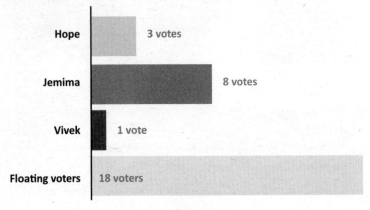

Dad says it's only the school council, not the presidential elections for the United States of America, and maybe I'm taking it a bit too seriously.

I reminded him that the school council is actually extremely serious, because as a school councillor, I would have the opportunity to change school policy on climate change and recycling, not to mention the lunch menu. He has promised to help me write my speech.

Finn hasn't written a single word of his speech, although he has drawn a big map of the Durdle Primary Water Park, including the Funnel Slide, the Terror Chute and the Pirate Ship (with fully-functional water cannons).

'They're never going to let you close the school and build a water park,' I told him. 'It's just silly.'

'You have to follow your dreams,' Finn said.

I haven't had a reply from Marcus Wilton yet, but it's only been one day. I know I need to be patient. Famous footballers probably don't have much time to reply to their messages.

FRIDAY 14 MARCH

The clock is ticking. Time is running out. For the planet. And for me.

There is only one more week till the school council elections. I can't wait. I wish the elections were today, not next Friday. I've already written my speech. I'm ready to win.

I asked Miss Brockenhurst if we could bring the elections forward by a week, but she said no, because that would be unfair on the other candidates. She said I'm just going to have to be patient.

Jemima came up to me in break.

'We need to talk,' she said.

'About what?'

'Your blog,' she said.

She has been reading my blog. I suppose she wanted to know more about her opponents in the elections.

'I'm not bossy,' Jemima said.

'I never said you were bossy.'

'Yes, you did. Here. On Monday the tenth of March.' She had printed out the page to prove she was right. 'I'd like you to delete this, please.'

'Fine,' I said. 'I did say you were bossy, but it's true, you *are* bossy. Ask anyone.'

Jemima didn't care. 'Even if it is true, which it isn't, you're not allowed to say that. It's cyber-bullying. So please delete it immediately.'

She's so bossy! But I don't want to be a cyber-bully.

If you're reading this, Jemima, I want you to know something: I am sorry about what I said, I shouldn't have said it. I didn't mean to be rude to you. I won't do it again, I promise.

At lunch I sat next to Vivek. We both had the vegetarian option, which was mung bean curry with rice and peas.

It wasn't spicy, which is good, because I don't like spicy food, but I would have preferred it to taste of something.

Vivek said I should come to his house and try his mum's curries, because they'll blow the top of my head off.

I said thanks, but no thanks.

Vivek is a Hindu and his family is vegetarian. They're not vegans. They drink milk and eat cheese, but they don't have any meat or fish.

Vivek has a brilliant idea. He wants his mum to come and help the dinner ladies come up with some new vegetarian recipes.

She always cooks vegetarian food for him and his sisters, but it's never tasteless, or nasty. It's always really delicious.

'You should tell Mr Khan,' I said. 'Or the dinner ladies.'

But he didn't want to. He felt embarrassed.

'Then *I* will,' I said.

We talked about the elections. I told him what Jemima had said about my blog.

'She'll be even more determined to beat you now,' Vivek said.

'I know,' I said, 'but I don't care. I'm determined to beat her too.'

Then I got a big surprise – Vivek is going to vote for me.

I couldn't understand why. Shouldn't he vote for himself? Doesn't he want to win?

Vivek said, 'I'm only doing the election because my mum said I had to.'

I thought that was really strange. Why did his mum want him to do the election if he didn't want to?

Vivek wasn't sure either. 'My mum's like that,' he said. 'I hope you win. You'd be a good school councillor – you really care about things and you have so many good ideas. You'd be much better than me. I think you'd be better than Jemima too. I'm definitely going to vote for you.' Which is very nice of him.

There are now four people voting for me: Harry, Selma, Vivek and me. So I only need eleven more votes to tie with Jemima or twelve if I'm going to beat her.

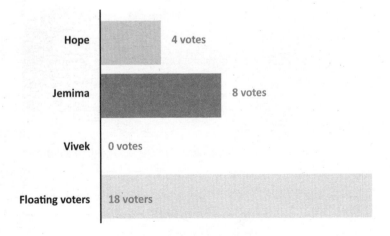

Hope 4 votes

Jemima 8 votes

Vivek 0 votes

Floating voters 18 voters

When I had finished my lunch, I had a chat with Mrs Darlington and Mrs Baptist. I told them what Vivek had suggested about his mum.

I thought they would be pleased to have some help and advice, but in fact they were even grumpier than usual.

Mrs Darlington said, 'We don't need anyone telling us how to do our jobs, young lady.'

Mrs Baptist said, 'We are both perfectly good cooks already, thank you very much.'

If you're wondering about Marcus Wilton, I can tell you he hasn't replied yet. Finn told me that he has an important match tomorrow. In fact, Finn won't stop talking about it. Perhaps he's very busy preparing for that.

Tonight Aunt Jess came over. She's not a vegetarian, which actually surprised me, because she loves animals, and she cares about the planet almost as much as me.

Aunt Jess said, 'I just can't resist the taste of meat. I feel bad about it, I wish I was different, but I can't help myself. If someone is frying bacon or roasting a chicken, I'll eat it.'

I said, 'You have to be strong.'

'I'm not,' Aunt Jess said. 'I'm weak. I can't resist meat. Mmmmmm. It's so delicious, I couldn't give it up.'

I said, 'What about the planet? Don't you care about climate change?'

'Of course I do,' Aunt Jess said.

'How much do you care about it?'

'A lot,' she said.

'Which do you care about more?' I said. 'Saving the planet? Or eating a burger?'

'The planet, of course.'

'If you really did,' I said, 'you'd give up eating meat. You'd stop

being a carnivore and become a vegan or a vegetarian.'

'I'm a flexitarian,' Aunt Jess said.

'A what?' I said.

'A flexitarian,' Aunt Jess repeated.

I had never heard of flexitarians, so Aunt Jess explained what they are. A flexitarian is sometimes vegetarian or vegan and sometimes a meat eater. A flexitarian might be vegetarian or vegan for a part of the week, or part of the day, and a meat-eater for a different part. Some flexitarians only eat meat at the weekend. Other flexitarians only eat meat after 6pm. Right now, for instance, Aunt Jess is a vegetarian for breakfast and lunch, but an omnivore in the evening.

'Basically it's a great way of reducing how much meat you eat without becoming a full-time vegan or vegetarian,' said Aunt Jess. 'You can save the planet and still eat the odd burger. Or a juicy raw steak. Or a tasty salmon fishcake. And all the other things which I would miss so much if I was veggie.'

I could have talked all night about vegans, vegetarians, pescatarians, omnivores, carnivores and flexitarians, but Mum stopped me.

'That's enough of this subject for one evening,' Mum said. 'Let Jess enjoy her food without making her feel guilty.'

So we stopped talking about climate change or what we should all be eating, and instead Aunt Jess told us about her dating disasters. I wish I could tell you about them too, because they are very funny. Unfortunately Aunt Jess made us promise not to breathe a word to anyone.

Hope Jones' Blog

SATURDAY 15 MARCH

Mitch has a new sign outside his shop.

I giggled when I saw that. Then I felt bad for laughing. What if someone ate Sparkle, or me? That wouldn't be very funny, would it?

Actually I was hoping to see Sparkle, but she wasn't protesting outside the shop. She was probably still in bed.

Mitch was very disappointed to hear I'm still a vegan. 'I'm all in favour of saving the planet,' Mitch said, 'but I don't see why I can't have the odd steak too.'

'Or chicken,' Mum said. She told him about flexitarians.

'They sound like very sensible people to me,' Mitch said nodding. 'Everything in moderation, that's my motto.' He wrapped up a chicken for Mum. Then he offered me another free sausage roll.

'No, thank you,' I said. 'Unless you have a vegan one.'

We went to Bosphorus to buy some vegetables and a big bag of rice. Then we got some nice bread from Katya at the bakery. Finally, we stopped for a snack in Flat White. I had a smoothie and Mum had a coffee, and we shared one of Brendan's famous macarons.

Sparkle was there! She was having a coffee with Tariq and Becca.

'I might go and protest later,' Sparkle said. 'I'm not feeling too great this morning.'

Becca said, 'She means it was a good party.'

'Too good,' Tariq said.

I'm glad they went to a good party. How very nice for them.

But what about saving the world? Isn't that more important than parties?

Becca says I'll feel differently when I'm a bit older.

I bet I won't.

Sparkle wanted to know if I'm a vegan now or just a vegetarian. I said a bit of both. Like Becca. Sometimes I eat some cheese or drink some milk, particularly at school, because the vegetarian lunches are vegetarian, not vegan. So I try to be vegan most days. But I don't always succeed.

'Like today,' Sparkle said.

I didn't understand what she was talking about until she pointed out that my macaron is made from eggs.

I did not know that.

I went to the counter and had a chat with Brendan. I suggested he should put signs on all his cakes and snacks, explaining the ingredients, so vegans and vegetarians know which ones are suitable. He thinks it's a great idea. He already has signs for allergies, so it won't be a big change for him.

He was very sorry to hear I couldn't eat my macaron. He gave me a vegan flapjack instead.

'This contains no animal products,' he said. 'That's a promise.'

He's going to find out if there's a way of making vegan macarons.

Apparently there are animal products everywhere, even in

things you'd never guess contained animals. For instance, did you know some soap is made from animals? Sparkle only buys vegan soap.

She said most chocolate bars aren't vegan, because they contain milk powder.

Some toothpaste is made with animal products. So is some food colouring, some beer, some wine, some pasta, some chewing gum and some sweets.

'Always check the label,' Sparkle said. 'If you're a vegan, you have to be very careful about what you buy.'

On the way home, we passed Mitch's shop again. He was inside, selling some steak to a man with a bright red face. They were talking so intensely that Mitch didn't even notice me. He didn't see me rubbing out the joke on his sign, and he didn't see me writing a new one.

Hope Jones' Blog

SUNDAY 16 MARCH

Help! There's a dead bird in our house!

Doesn't it look disgusting? Why would anyone want to eat that? Looking at it made me happy to be a vegan. I just wish the rest of my family felt the same way.

Mum and Dad keep sniffing the air and saying how delicious it smells. Finn can't wait for lunch.

'He's a growing boy,' Mum said. 'He needs his protein.'

I reminded her that there is more than enough protein in spinach, beans and lentils.

'We'll have spinach and beans tomorrow,' Mum said. 'Today we're having roast chicken. You should be proud of me, Hope. This was a very expensive chicken. Free-range. Organic. It's led a happy life.'

'It would be even happier if it was still alive,' I pointed out.

Even Becca wants some chicken today. She's getting a cold, so she needs the extra energy.

I still haven't had a reply from Marcus Wilton, which is extremely frustrating. I wrote to him three days ago. I'm beginning to think he might never write back. Finn says he won his important game on Saturday, so he might have been too busy celebrating.

Before lunch, while the chicken was in the oven, I made my poster for the school council elections.

Becca helped me. She was in a good mood because her date with Tariq was so great. He took her to another party, which was even better than the one on Friday.

Becca is brilliant at art. When she grows up, she's going to be a graphic designer. Her favourite artists are Salvador Dalí and Frida Kahlo. I didn't know anything about either of them, but Becca has been showing me their pictures, and I have to admit they're very interesting.

She used them as inspiration for my poster. First she made one in the style of Salvador Dalí.

But it wasn't quite right. I didn't think it would make anyone vote for me. So she made another in the style of Frida Kahlo.

That wasn't quite right either.

'Back to the drawing board,' Becca said. She did some doodles, then she searched on the internet. Suddenly she shouted, 'Got it!'

Being artistic is like that. Sometimes you can't think of anything, you are completely stuck, your mind is blank, you think you'll never be able to create anything. And then, just when you're about to give up and do something else instead, inspiration strikes. That's what Becca says, anyway.

She grabbed a pencil. She ran to her room to find a different sketchbook. Then she scribbled and scribbled before turning the page to show me.

HOPE

Vote for Hope Jones as your representative on the school council.

'What do you think?' Becca said.

'I love it,' I said.

I hope you love it too. And obviously I hope everyone in my class loves it, so they vote for me in the school council elections.

Dad is going to print out fifty copies at work tomorrow. He says the IT department won't mind. Then I'm going to put up the posters all around school.

For my lunch, I had potatoes, carrots, peas, cabbage and a nut roast, which Mum had made especially for me.

'You can have some chicken if you want,' Finn said.

'I'd rather not,' I said.

'You're missing out,' Finn said. 'This is yummy.'

'So is this,' I said.

'It looks gross.'

'It tastes great,' I said.

You know what? It really did.

MONDAY 17 MARCH

Jemima Higginbotham brought her posters to school today. Miss Brockenhurst has already pinned them up in our classroom.

I don't like saying this, but they look amazing. They were designed by someone who works in her dad's company and printed by a professional printer. Jemima also made badges for everyone in the class and recorded a personal statement which you can watch on the internet.

Finn said everyone in his class wants to vote for me, which is

very nice of them. Unfortunately they can't. You can only vote for someone in your own class. He doesn't think they're going to vote for him instead, despite me being his big sister.

Mum thinks I don't even need posters, let alone badges or a movie on the internet. She thinks people will vote for me because of my ideas and my passion, not my posters.

I wish she was right. Unfortunately, I don't think people care about ideas or passion. They're more interested in posters and badges.

When Dad came home from work, I said, 'Where are my posters?'

He said, 'Your what?'

Apparently today had been super-busy at work, because Trevor broke his ankle playing five-a-side over the weekend, so they've been sharing out his workload.

I'm very sorry to hear about Trevor's ankle. But I do wish Dad had remembered my posters. I've set an alarm on his phone to remind him to print them tomorrow. He'd better not forget again or I will be seriously upset.

If you're reading this, Dad: please print my posters!

TUESDAY 18 MARCH

The school council elections are on Friday, and we're spending the whole week learning about democracy. It has been really interesting so far. I already knew about Emmeline Pankhurst and the fight for women's suffrage, but there were a lot of other facts which I didn't know.

For instance, do you know the difference between a democracy and a dictatorship?

I didn't.

But now I do.

DEMOCRACY

The people vote for the government.

DICTATORSHIP

The dictator makes the rules and imposes them on the people.

Miss Brockenhurst asked us a question: 'Which is better, a democracy or a dictatorship?'

Obviously I would prefer to live in a democracy, unless I was the dictator. That was my answer. Dictatorships are good for dictators, but democracies are better for everyone else.

Miss Brockenhurst agreed with me.

Harry put up his hand to ask a question. Actually, it wasn't a question. It was more of a statement: 'We live in a dictatorship,' he said.

'No, you don't,' said Miss Brockenhurst. 'Our country is a democracy. Our ancestors fought for their right to vote.'

'I'm not talking about this country,' Harry said. 'I'm talking about this school.'

Miss Brockenhurst was beginning to look a bit worried.

Harry explained what he meant: 'We don't get to vote,' he said. 'We just have to do what we're told to, by you, and the other teachers. So it's not a democracy, is it? This is a dictatorship, and you just said dictatorships are terrible.'

'You do get to vote for the school council,' Miss Brockenhurst pointed out.

'The school council can't decide very much,' Harry replied. 'If this was a real democracy, we would have votes on everything. We would vote on the school rules. We could vote if we wanted to wear a uniform or just our normal clothes. We could vote about what to learn. But we can't vote about anything important, can we? We just have to do what you tell us, so doesn't that mean we live in a dictatorship?'

Miss Brockenhurst said Harry asks very interesting questions and that's why he's such a pleasure to teach. But she didn't actually answer his question or explain why dictatorships are fine if they're schools, but not so good if they're whole countries.

In break I talked to Clementine and Gwen in my class. They both want to vote for me, but one thing is stopping them.

I said, 'What is it?'

They didn't want to tell me, but I persuaded them.

Jemima Higginbotham has been promising to buy a bag of lollipops for anyone who votes for her.

That is outrageous! Miss Brockenhurst was very clear that bribery is strictly forbidden. I am going to make an official complaint.

I talked to Tom too. He still hasn't decided who to vote for. He really likes Vivek and his ideas. He would be happy if we spent all our time playing football at school, or talking about football, or thinking about football.

I explained it's not exactly realistic.

He said, 'It's just as realistic as you saving the world.' Which shows he hasn't been listening to me. I'm not saying I'm going to save the world on my own. I'm saying we can all save the world if we work together. That's the whole point! It's not a dictatorship, it's a democracy. I won't tell everyone what to do, we'll all do it together. Me and Tom and Gwen and Clementine. And you too. Together we're going to save the world.

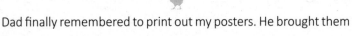

Dad finally remembered to print out my posters. He brought them home after work. Thanks, Dad! I'll take them to school tomorrow.

WEDNESDAY 19 MARCH

I took my posters to school this morning. Miss Brockenhurst said fifty was a little excessive, because every class is electing a school councillor, and what would happen if every candidate wanted to pin up fifty posters around the school? She suggested I put a couple in the classroom and a couple more on the board in the corridor outside, then she took two for the staff room.

Selma and I put some posters in the girls' toilets while Harry put some in the boys'. Then we pinned two more to the wall in the playground.

I've got thirty-seven posters left. I've put them in my tray for now. I'm sure they'll come in useful.

I've also been talking to everyone in my class. Eden and Tom have promised they're going to vote for me, which makes six altogether.

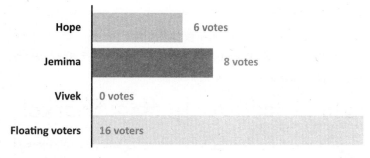

Everyone else says they're waiting to hear our speeches. Mine will just have to be brilliant.

I worked on it after school. I don't want to be arrogant, but I think it's quite good. My family agreed.

I did my speech for Dad when he came back from work. He was very tired after a day at the office, so he wanted to collapse on the sofa with a quiet beer, but he still managed to give me some useful feedback. He thinks I need some pictures. He sits through a lot of presentations at work and apparently they're a bit less boring with pictures.

Finn claims to have finished his speech, although he's only actually written five words on a piece of paper:

Big slides! Pirate ship! Sharks!

I explained that a real speech needs a beginning, a middle and an end – not to mention facts, illustrations, persuasive language and preferably a few jokes – but Finn didn't care.

'It doesn't have to be complicated,' he said. 'I just want to build a water park with some great slides and a pirate ship.'

'What about the sharks?' I asked.

'Those are for people who don't behave,' he said. 'Or annoy me.'

He really needs to take the school council more seriously if he wants to be elected. 'You'll never convince anyone to vote for you,' I told him. 'You need to work harder and write a better speech.'

'I'm too busy,' he said. Although he was actually just playing with Lego.

The elections are the day after tomorrow. He'd better get a move on or his class will have elected someone else before he's even had a chance to write his speech.

Tonight Tariq came round to our house and made his famous stew. (His stew isn't really famous, but it is extremely tasty.) He brought onions, aubergines, spinach, tomatoes, rice and a bag of fresh spices which made the whole house smell amazing.

tariq

326 likes

tariq I've been cooking vegan food with my friend Hope. We love animals, so we don't want to eat them. And we're being kind to the planet. **#govegan #savetheplanet #chefsagainstclimatechange #hopejonessavestheworld #plantpower**

THURSDAY 20 MARCH

I'm worried that Jemima is going to beat me in the elections. Half the people in our class are wearing her badges. In fact, half the people in the school are wearing her badges.

I'll just have to give a brilliant speech and persuade my class with the power of my arguments.

Harry has been doing some more research for me. I'm definitely going to use some of his statistics in my speech. They are very persuasive. He's found several great pictures too.

Harry doesn't want to become a vegetarian or a vegan, because he likes meat too much, and he loves fish. But he is willing to cut down on his meat consumption, because he cares about the planet. So he is going to be a flexitarian like Aunt Jess.

He talked to his mum and dad, and they would also like to become flexitarians. They've decided to make another change too: they are only going to buy meat which hasn't come from factory farms.

Harry has worked out that although they're not actually giving up meat altogether, they will make a significant difference to their overall meat consumption.

 The Murakami family:
Meat eating options, a weekly survey.

>> 3 people x 1 week = 21 days total

OPTION ONE

- Harry gives up meat and becomes vegetarian =
  **7 NO-MEAT DAYS
  0 MEAT DAYS**

- Harry's Mum and Dad eat meat =
  **0 NO-MEAT DAYS
  14 MEAT DAYS**

Weekly total: 7 no-meat days / 14 meat days

OPTION TWO

- Harry eats meat only at weekends =
  **5 NO-MEAT DAYS
  2 MEAT DAYS**

- Harry's Mum and Dad eat meat only at weekends =
  **10 NO-MEAT DAYS
  4 MEAT DAYS**

Weekly Total: 15 no-meat days / 6 meat days

I found Harry's sums a bit complicated, but after he had explained them to me three times, I understood what he meant. Then he did the sums for my family too.

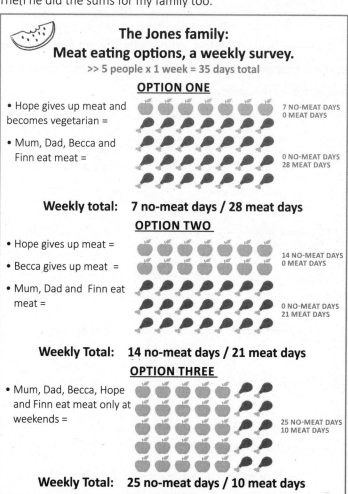

The Jones family:
Meat eating options, a weekly survey.
>> 5 people x 1 week = 35 days total

OPTION ONE

- Hope gives up meat and becomes vegetarian =

- Mum, Dad, Becca and Finn eat meat =

7 NO-MEAT DAYS
0 MEAT DAYS

0 NO-MEAT DAYS
28 MEAT DAYS

Weekly total: 7 no-meat days / 28 meat days

OPTION TWO

- Hope gives up meat =

- Becca gives up meat =

- Mum, Dad and Finn eat meat =

14 NO-MEAT DAYS
0 MEAT DAYS

0 NO-MEAT DAYS
21 MEAT DAYS

Weekly Total: 14 no-meat days / 21 meat days

OPTION THREE

- Mum, Dad, Becca, Hope and Finn eat meat only at weekends =

25 NO-MEAT DAYS
10 MEAT DAYS

Weekly Total: 25 no-meat days / 10 meat days

If my whole family became flexitarians, we would eat less meat than just me becoming a vegan and the others remaining as carnivores.

It's the same for everyone at school. I'm not saying everyone has to become vegetarians or vegans. But if we all became flexitarians, we would make a huge difference to the planet.

I'd better go, I've got to practise my speech. The school council elections are tomorrow. I'm very nervous!

Finn still hasn't written his speech.

If you're reading this, and you're in my class, please remember to vote tomorrow! Obviously I'm not going to tell you who to vote for, that's your choice, but my policies are extremely fair and sensible. And will make the world a better place.

If you're reading this, and you're not in my class, please wish me luck.

FRIDAY 21 MARCH

Today has been incredible.

The actual meaning of 'incredible' is 'impossible to believe'. That is exactly what today has been. I'll tell you all about it.

This morning we held the elections for the school council. First there were the hustings, which is when the candidates speak to the electorate and explain why they should be elected. We drew straws, Jemima got the shortest so she went first, then Vivek, and finally me.

Jemima was really good. She talked about democracy. She said we are only kids, but we're still humans and we have rights. Why should we have to do homework when we spent so much time working at school already? Shouldn't we be allowed to relax? Can't we have some time at home to do our own stuff like make art and be creative?

She made some very good points about getting a class pet. She said animals are proven to be beneficial to children's mental health and well-being, and each class should definitely get its own pet, because having all these animals in the school will make us healthier and happier and better learners.

She said the pet doesn't have to be a dog or a cat, or even a rabbit. It could be a stick insect or a gerbil.

She said wet play is usually very boring, so wouldn't it be better if we spent our time more usefully? Then she made several excellent suggestions about pen licences. When she finished, everyone clapped for ages.

I was getting nervous.

Vivek was brilliant too. He has passionate views about children's need for physical exercise.

Vivek promised that if we spend more time running around and less time sitting at our desks, we will sleep better, feel better, and grow up to be bigger, stronger and much healthier. Everyone clapped him for ages too.

By this point I was so nervous I was actually shaking.

'Your turn, Hope,' said Miss Brockenhurst.

I stood up and went to the front of the class. I felt like running away, but I managed to give my speech without messing it up.

| | Tweets 1400 | Following 620 | Followers 1366 | Likes 906 |

Durdle Primary School
We love learning. This term's values are persistence and resilience

Tweet   Message

Today we have been electing the school council. Otters class had three fabulous speeches from their candidates. #schooldemocracy #pupilpower #Durdlehero

Hello, I'm Hope.

Obviously you know that already.

I would like to be on the school council for three reasons:

One: I am a good listener.

Two: I am a good communicator.

Three: There are things about the school that I want to change.

I'll say a little more about each of these three.

Firstly, I am a good listener, so if anyone had good ideas, I would listen to them, and make sure they weren't forgotten. I would be good at representing all our ideas to the school.

Secondly, I am a good communicator, so I would be good at expressing these ideas to our teachers, and persuading them to act on them. I would be good at mediating between us and Mr Khan and the rest of the teachers.

Thirdly, I have ideas of my own.

I just want to mention one of them that I feel passionately about.

Climate change.

Our school should be taking a lead in making things better and saving the planet. Climate change is going to effect all our lives.

As children, we can't do much. We can't change laws or even vote. But we can ask our parents to change their behaviour. By getting out of their cars and walking, for instance, or taking fewer flights. And we can ask the school to change its behaviour too.

The school could do more reusing and recycling. We could reduce our consumption. We could stop using single-use plastic. We could stop eating meat. We could stop consuming animal products like cheese and milk and eggs.

Did you know that farming is the biggest single cause of global emissions?

Animals cause a huge amount of pollution, mainly by farting and burping.

I know it's funny, but they do fart and burp a lot. Their farts and burps cause a huge amount of emissions, contributing to climate change.

We could make a big difference if we ate less meat.

I'm not saying you have to become a vegetarian, but can't you eat a bit less meat? Do you really have to eat animals or birds three times a day? I don't think so, which is why I think this school should become vegetarian.

You can still have bacon for breakfast or a burger for tea. But let's all be vegetarian at lunchtime. That would make a big difference. Think about all the children in this school – there are almost five hundred of us; it takes a lot of chickens, cows and pigs to feed us all. If this school was vegetarian, think of all the chickens, cows and pigs who wouldn't have to be killed!

Quite soon Miss Brockenhurst is going to hand out the voting papers and we'll all get a chance to vote.

I hope you'll vote for me. If you do, and I am elected to the school council, I can't promise I will save the world, but I will try.

A vote for me is a vote for a better future.

Thank you.

After all three of us had finished our speeches, we sat down again, and Miss Brockenhurst handed out pieces of paper for the vote.

We had a secret ballot, which means you make a tick next to the name of the person you want to vote for on your ballot paper, then fold it in half and put it in a cardboard box. No one knows who you voted for.

Durdle Primary
School Council Elections
Friday March 21st

Your candidates are:

Jemima HIGGINBOTHAM ☐

Vivek SIDHU ☐

Hope JONES ☐

Please tick only ONE box.

Then fold your slip in half and place in the ballot box.

Before we did the actual voting, Miss Brockenhurst gave a little speech herself.

'This is a democracy,' she said. 'Everyone has one vote. I want you to use your vote wisely. You've heard from the three candidates, you know about their ideas, now you have to choose. Who would represent you best? Who would you like to speak for this class on the school council? You only have one vote, so please think carefully before you make your choice.'

I didn't know who to vote for. Me? Or one of the others?

I didn't really like the idea of voting for myself, it felt wrong. On the other hand, I needed every vote I could get because I wanted to win. And I thought – *I should win, my ideas are important. If I am elected to the school council, I will help to make the world a better place. I won't just make promises I can't keep, like banning homework or everyone doing sports instead of lessons.*

It was a very difficult dilemma, I felt pulled in both directions. I still hadn't made up my mind when Miss Brockenhurst said, 'Has everyone finished? Because I'm going to collect the ballots now.'

I would have liked a bit more time to think carefully, but I knew I had to tick a box. Quickly. So I ticked the one marked Hope JONES.

As soon as I had made my decision, Miss Brockenhurst collected my ballot paper.

Miss Brockenhurst put all the ballot papers in a cardboard box. Then she told us to get our books from our trays and read while she counted the votes.

I got my book, but I couldn't read, I was too excited.

Miss Brockenhurst counted the votes, then she counted them again to make sure. It was very tense. Finally she told us to put down our books so she could announce the result.

	Tweets	Following	Followers	Likes
	1421	621	1371	912

Durdle Primary School
We love learning. This term's values are persistence and resilience

Tweet   Message

Miss Brockenhurst counts the school council votes in Otters Class #schooldemocracy #pupilpower #Durdlehero

VOTE

'Congratulations to all three candidates,' Miss Brockenhurst said. 'This has been a fantastic contest. Thank you to our three brilliant candidates — Jemima, Vivek, and Hope. You all gave wonderful speeches. You have clearly been working very hard and thinking deeply about ways to improve the school. Your efforts have inspired everyone. I've now counted the votes, and I can tell you that the contest was extremely close. I wish all three of you could be elected to the school council. Unfortunately, there can only be one winner. This year, our class representative for the school council is . . .'

She left a long pause.

And then she said: ' . . . Vivek.'

I clapped with everyone else. I tried to smile, but inside I felt terrible.

Vivek?

Vivek??

Vivek????????????

Why would anyone vote for him? Why didn't they vote for me?

SATURDAY 22 MARCH

How am I supposed to change the world if no one will vote for me? I am just one person. I can't do it alone.

Mum keeps telling me to look on the bright side. She says I must have saved several animals already by not eating them, and think how grateful they must be. She says the planet would be grateful too, if planets had emotions.

I know she's trying to be nice, but for some reason it just makes me feel more depressed. Yes, she's right, I've probably saved a chicken and a few fish by becoming vegan, but think how many animals have died to feed my school! Think how many could have been saved if I had been elected to the school council!

I've been trying to work out what I could have done differently. Should I have written a better speech? Or made nicer posters? I really don't know.

Finn won his election. He is going to be on the school council. His class voted for him by a huge majority.

I couldn't believe it. 'What about your speech?' I said.

'They liked it,' he said.

'But it was only five words!'

'That was one of the things they liked,' he said. 'It didn't go on too long.'

Aunt Jess came over this morning. She brought some vegan croissants to cheer me up. They weren't as crumbly or tasty as ordinary croissants, because they contained no butter.

Perhaps that's why I didn't really enjoy them. Or perhaps I'm just too sad to enjoy food at the moment. Even croissants, which I usually love.

After breakfast, Dad and Finn went to football practice.

I wanted to spend the morning at home, but Mum wouldn't let me. She said, 'You're not allowed to stay in the house on your own. You can come shopping with us.'

'I'm not alone,' I said. 'Becca's here.'

'She's fast asleep.'

'I could shout at her if I had a problem.'

'Come with us,' Aunt Jess said. 'It'll be fun.'

'The fresh air will make you feel better,' Mum said.

You know what? They were both wrong. It wasn't fun, and the fresh air didn't make me feel any different. The shops actually made me more miserable.

Sparkle wasn't protesting outside Mitch's shop. The teenagers all went to another party last night, so she was probably still in bed.

Mum bought sausages for the whole family. Except me and Becca, of course.

Aunt Jess said to Mitch, 'Have you met my niece? Do you know she's a vegan?'

'She's been trying to persuade me to become one too,' Mitch said. 'I could be the first vegan butcher in history.'

'That certainly would be a unique selling point,' Aunt Jess said. 'Although I don't know if I'd buy a steak from a man who wouldn't eat it himself.'

'That's what I'm worried about,' Mitch said. 'Actually, Hope, I've been thinking about this all week and I've finally worked out the answer. Do you want to know why I think it's right for humans to eat animals?'

'Not really,' I said.

I didn't feel like arguing with Mitch. I just wanted to go back to bed and pull the duvet over my head. Maybe I'm becoming a teenager.

Aunt Jess says I'm doing my best, and no one can do more than that, and she admires me for trying so hard, which is very nice of her, but I still feel depressed. Actually, I feel too depressed to write my blog. So I'm going to stop now.

Hope Jones' Blog

MONDAY 24 MARCH

Mondays are my days for cooking with Dad now. Today he bought all the ingredients for lentil soup.

I didn't feel like cooking. I just wanted to lie on the sofa with Poppadom and watch some TV. So I said, 'Can you make it without me?'

'That's not the deal,' Dad said. 'The deal is we make it together.'

'I don't feel like making anything,' I said.

'Cooking will cheer you up,' Dad promised.

I didn't believe him, but do you know what? He was right.

I had never made lentil soup before, so I felt a bit nervous, but it was surprisingly easy. And very tasty.

hope

19 likes

hope Today I made lentil soup. It was scrum-diddly-umptious! Just fry an onion with some celery and carrot. Add garlic and some salt. You could also add some ginger and herbs if you like them. When the veggies are nice and soft, add some lentils and water. Bring to the boil. Turn down to a simmer. Leave it to bubble away for half an hour. Serve with toast and a dollop of yoghurt.

#homecooking #savetheplanet #ilovelentils #meatfreeMondays
#hopejonessavestheworld

TUESDAY 25 MARCH

Everyone is still talking about the school council elections. Harry voted for me, I knew he would. So did Selma, like she'd promised. So did Vivek, like he said he would. He already knew I hadn't voted for him, because he's been reading my blog. (Hi, Vivek!) He thinks I was right to vote for myself and he wishes I had won, not him.

'I only stood for the school council because my mum insisted,' he said. 'She said it would be a good experience. I don't know what for. I don't want to be a politician, I can't think of anything worse.'

People are so different, aren't they? I would love to be a politician. I can't think of anything better.

'You should really be on the school council,' Vivek said. 'You'd be brilliant, not like me, I'll be terrible. I don't know why I won.'

'Because everyone voted for you,' I said.

'They shouldn't have,' Vivek said. 'I don't know why they did.'

'Because you're nice and your speech was really good. You do care a lot about playing sport,' I explained to him. 'Also, maybe they liked your ideas more than mine? They want to play different sports. They'd rather do football instead of lessons.'

I asked Gwen who she had voted for. At first, she didn't want to tell me.

I said, 'Are you embarrassed?'

She said, 'No.'

'Did you make a mistake?'

'No.'

'Then why don't you want to tell me?'

'I don't want to upset anyone,' Gwen said.

I told her not to worry. The vote is over, life goes on, no one is going to be upset, whoever she might have voted for.

But I was wrong. When she told me, I was upset. And very, very confused.

This is what Gwen told me: she wanted to vote for me, because she likes me, and she cares about saving the world; but she also wanted to vote for Jemima because she is one of Jemima's seven best friends, and she loves the bracelet that Jemima gave her.

She couldn't choose between us, so she voted for Vivek, which is bizarre because she doesn't even like sport!

Maybe democracy isn't the best way to run things. Maybe dictatorships *are* better.

If I was the dictator, I would just tell everyone how to save the world. They'd have to do it whether or not they wanted to. They might not like that, but at least the world would get saved.

Hope Jones' Blog

WEDNESDAY 26 MARCH

I'm feeling much better today. I have had two very nice messages.

The first was from Granny. She's been reading my blog, and she was inspired by Monday's recipe, so she made lentil soup for Grandad. He loved it.

The second message was from Marcus Wilton.

Yes! That's right! Marcus Wilton – one of the most famous young footballers in the country, and probable winner of the Golden Boot at the next World Cup, if not the one after that!

I had actually given up on him, I thought he had never got my message or was too busy to reply.

Finn couldn't believe it. He said, 'Is this real? You actually got a message from *the* Marcus Wilton?'

'Marcus and I are old friends,' I said.

'Really?'

'No,' I admitted. 'But he has written to me. And, look, he's sent you a picture.'

FROM Marcus Wilton
TO Hope Jones
DATE Wednesday 26 March
SUBJECT Re: Meat and my brother
ATTACHMENTS My mum's curry

Hi Hope! Hi Finn!

Thanks for your great letter.

Let me tell you something: I am a proud vegan! Yes, that's right. I'm not a vegetarian. I am actually a vegan. I have completely given up all animal products.

In the old days, footballs and boots used to be made from animal products, but they're not any more. You can be a footballer without ever causing any pain or suffering to animals.

If you both want to be vegans, you'll have to be careful about your diet. You need to eat the right vitamins and stuff, because you're still growing.

Because I'm a professional athlete, I am careful to eat lots of protein and I take some special supplements which give me what I need. I'm fit and strong and completely healthy. All the doctors say so.

Here is a picture of me eating the best veggie curry in the world, made by the best cook in the world – my mum. It's stuffed with vitamins and protein. This is my favourite meal after a match. It tastes even better if I scored a goal (or three). You can find the recipe on my official website. Enjoy!

Marcus

For Finn,

from Marcus

FROM Hope Jones
TO Marcus Wilton
DATE Wednesday 26 March
SUBJECT RE: RE: Meat and my brother
ATTACHMENTS My brother Finn

Dear Marcus

You have been my brother's hero for a long time. Now you're my hero too.

Thank you for writing to Finn! You have changed how he feels about eating meat. He's not actually going to be a vegan. Or even a vegetarian. But he is going to become a flexitarian. In other words, he will try to eat less meat.

Your mum's veggie curry looks delicious. I'm definitely going to make it for Finn. (And me, obviously.)

Good luck on Saturday.

I hope you score lots of goals.

Yours sincerely

Hope Jones

Hope Jones' Blog

THURSDAY 27 MARCH

Today I had a very interesting conversation with Miss Brockenhurst. She asked me to stay behind before lunch. I was worried I'd done something wrong, but she actually just wanted to talk about the elections.

'I was impressed by your speech,' she said. 'It was a good example of persuasive writing.'

I felt a bit embarrassed, but pleased too. I just wish everyone else had felt the same way. If my speech was such a good example of persuasive writing, why weren't more people persuaded? Why did they all vote for Vivek?

Miss Brockenhurst didn't know the answers to those questions. But she did want to tell me something else.

'You take things very seriously,' she said to me. 'That's a good thing, of course it is, but not everybody feels the same way as you, Hope. Not everyone thinks so much about things, or cares so much. I admire your persistence and your dedication, I really do, but I hope it doesn't make you unhappy.'

I didn't want to tell her, but I am a bit unhappy. I really wanted to be elected to the school council. How am I supposed to save the world on my own?

Then Miss Brockenhurst told me something very surprising. She is a vegetarian! She has been since she was fourteen.

She said she has been vegan for some periods of her life, but not any more, mainly because she has a French boyfriend who refuses to give up cheese, and who could resist a sliver of Roquefort when it's sitting on the shelf in the fridge?

It was really interesting. I didn't know Miss Brockenhurst even had a boyfriend, especially not one from France. I wonder what he looks like.

Miss Brockenhurst gave me a couple of recipes which she said I might enjoy. She doesn't eat the school dinners. She brings in her own homemade salads and sandwiches, which she eats in the staff room.

I wish I could do that too, but we're not allowed packed lunches.

'I'd like to cook my own lunches,' I said. 'My friend Sparkle gave me a brilliant vegetarian cookery book. I've been using it to make lots of good recipes. I don't want to be rude to Mrs Darlington and Mrs Baptist, but I actually think I'm better at making vegetarian meals than they are.'

'I'm sure they do their best,' Miss Brockenhurst said. Then she had a brilliant idea. 'Why don't you lend them your cookery book? They could get some ideas for recipes.'

I'm going to bring it to school tomorrow.

I wanted to talk more about being a vegetarian with Miss Brockenhurst, and maybe even ask the name of her French boyfriend, but she said I was already late for lunch.

I had one last question for her. 'If you were voting in the school

council elections last week,' I said, 'who would you have voted for: Jemima, Vivek, or me?'

Miss Brockenhurst refused to answer the question. She said we were all very good candidates, and each of us deserved to win, and in a perfect world we would all be on the school council.

'But if you had to choose . . .' I said.

'Luckily I didn't have to,' Miss Brockenhurst said. 'Now, go to lunch. Quick! Or you'll miss your break.'

My conversation with Miss Brockenhurst has made me realise something – I couldn't persuade my class to vote for me, they wanted dreams instead of reality. They wanted to vote for abolishing lessons and playing football all day, rather than thinking about what will really happen to us, and the real changes that we have to make. Fine, that is their choice.

But I feel differently. I care about the future, I care about climate change, I care about our planet. I'll have to do something myself. But what?

Hope Jones' Blog

FRIDAY 28 MARCH

Before we went to school, I wrapped up my cookbook, so it looked like a proper present.

Mum reminded me to be tactful when I gave it to Mrs Darlington and Mrs Baptist, because I didn't want them to think I was criticising their cooking or telling them how to do their jobs.

So when I gave it to them, I just said it was a present to say thank you for all their nice lunches.

I thought they might be cross again, but they were actually really pleased.

Mrs Darlington said no one had ever given them a present before. 'Usually all we get is complaints,' she said.

'Half the kids don't even bother saying thank you,' said Mrs Baptist. 'Except every other Tuesday, when dessert is chocolate sponge.'

They're going to read my cookbook this weekend and get some inspiration for new vegetarian recipes.

I've asked them to make vegetarian lasagne. Sev puri would be nice too.

Have you ever eaten a sev puri?

I hadn't until today. In fact, I'd never even heard of them, but now I think they might be my favourite food.

Vivek invited me for tea after school. I think he must have been feeling guilty about the school council.

'I wish I hadn't won,' he said. 'I didn't want to.'

I told him not to worry. It's not his fault, he can't help how people voted.

Vivek said, 'I was sure no one would vote for me. It's pointless anyway, we're never going to have games all day, the school won't get rid of lessons.'

'They might,' I said.

But I knew he was right, of course they won't. Our school isn't really a democracy, it's a dictatorship, and Mr Khan is the dictator. He's always telling everyone what to do.

'Maybe you'll be able to change something,' I said. 'Maybe you could persuade Mr Khan to put on a sports day every term, instead of just once a year. Or to do lots of different sports. Or to play more tournaments with other schools.'

'That would be great,' Vivek said. 'Could you ask him?'

'You can ask him,' I said. 'You're on the school council.'

The first school council meeting is on Monday.

Vivek said, 'Do I really have to stand up and say I think we should abolish lessons and play football instead? Everyone will laugh at me.'

I advised him to say what he really does think.

Vivek looked worried. 'I don't know what I think.'

'You must know what you think,' I said.

'I'm not like you,' he said. 'I don't really have opinions about things.'

'You do have opinions,' I said. 'You like football and cricket, that's an opinion. And you think the vegetarian options for school lunches aren't very nice, that's an opinion too.'

Vivek agreed I was right. He promised to try and give some of his opinions at the school council next week. He'll tell them about his love of football and cricket, and his wish for us to play more games. And if they laugh at him – who cares?

His mum called us downstairs for tea. She had made a special meal because I was coming round.

I didn't even know what most of the things were; I'd never seen them before. Vivek told me all the different names. His mum wanted to explain how she made them, but his dad said, 'Let's not talk about the food too much. Just eat it, try it, see what you like.'

'What if she doesn't like anything?' Vivek said.

'Then she can have a cheese sandwich,' his dad said, 'or a bowl of cornflakes.'

Luckily the food was amazing. The best were the sev puri. Wow – they were so spicy! They made my mouth explode, but in a nice way.

Mango chutney

Gobi masala

Cucumber raita

Chapati

Onion bhaji

Dhal

Sparkle has asked me to go and protest outside Mitch's shop tomorrow morning. She's been making a new banner.

I said yes. I asked Becca and Finn if they would like to come too. Finn wasn't interested. He has football practice on Saturday mornings, and he wouldn't want to miss that for anything – even saving the world.

Becca promised to come with me if she's awake in time. 'But you'd better not wake me up,' she said. 'You know how much I need my lie-ins at the weekends.'

SATURDAY 29 MARCH

Today I had a big surprise, Aunt Jess gave it to me. First thing this morning, she came to pick me up. 'We're going on a little expedition,' she said.

Joe and Mo came out of their house to stare at her car. They asked if Aunt Jess would take them on a drive.

'Maybe another time,' she said. 'Right now, I need Hope to hurry up and grab her stuff, we don't want to be late.'

'Late for what?' I asked.

'The surprise,' Aunt Jess said.

Aunt Jess refused to tell me where we were going. All she would say is: 'You have to pack a small suitcase, just enough for one night, and you need a change of clothes and a toothbrush. Oh, and you'd better bring some wellies.'

Obviously it wasn't a surprise to Mum and Dad. Aunt Jess had arranged it with them in advance. She wanted to cheer me up because I had been feeling so sad.

I said, 'Where are you taking me?'

'You'll have to wait and see,' Aunt Jess said.

'That's not fair! You have to tell me!'

'No way,' she said. 'Then it wouldn't be a surprise.'

Where could she be taking me? Why would I need a toothbrush and my wellies?

I had no idea, but I packed them anyway, and said goodbye to Mum and Dad.

Finn wanted to come too, but Mum said not this time. 'Today is just for Hope.'

I texted Sparkle and explained why I couldn't protest outside Mitch's shop.

> I'm very sorry. I can't come to the protest today. I'm going to a secret destination with my aunt Jess.

> What's your secret destination? Tell me more!

> I don't know yet because it's a secret but I'll tell you when I do.

> Sounds exciting. Don't worry about the protest. Actually I can't go either.

> Why not?

> Still in bed! Let's do it next week instead.

Once we started driving, I begged Aunt Jess to tell me about the secret destination, but she wouldn't.

She did tell me one thing – she had arranged it with Mitch.

I was amazed. I didn't even know she and Mitch were friends, but apparently they've been seeing one another recently after I introduced them.

'So where are we going?' I asked.

'Wait and see.' Aunt Jess said.

We drove for ages. First on the motorway. Then through the countryside. Until we finally arrived at our secret destination.

It's so beautiful here.

And so clean!

I can breathe!

I can't smell any fumes or pollution.

I can smell a lot of poo, but for some reason it doesn't smell too bad. It actually smells quite nice.

It turns out we have come to meet Mitch's friends, Robert and Caroline. They're farmers, who supply some of the meat in Mitch's shop.

Robert and Caroline have three children — Dotty, Viv, and Ben— and two dogs, Pepper and George, who are the most obedient and well-trained dogs in the world. They do whatever Robert says.

Actually, that's not true. He doesn't even need to *say* anything. He issues all his instructions by whistling, and the dogs know exactly what he wants. It's amazing to watch.

Robert and Caroline have hundreds of sheep, who are having babies at the moment. The lambs are so sweet!

Robert and Caroline also have twenty hens, who just wander around all day, pecking the earth, searching for corn and seeds.

Every night they're locked up in the barn so they don't get eaten by foxes. No one knows exactly where the hens are going to lay their eggs, so you have to search for them. I found two: the first was hidden under a cardboard box in the barn, the other was just sitting in the straw.

Robert said I could have scrambled eggs for breakfast tomorrow.

I said, thanks, but no thanks. I didn't want to be rude so I explained why. 'I'm a vegan,' I said, 'because I want to save the world.'

I told Robert my reasons for not eating meat.

Robert listened to me very carefully. Then he said, 'I don't think these eggs would make a difference to climate change. The hens aren't using any extra resources, they're just pecking the seeds and worms in the earth which would be there anyway. The hens do poo, but their poo actually acts as a fertiliser, helping more plants to grow. They probably don't fart much either.'

'Or burp,' I said.

'Or burp,' Robert agreed.

We had a very interesting conversation about climate change. Robert is actually quite an expert. He knows much more than me. He probably knows more than Sparkle too. He told me all about deforestation and conservation and good practice and modern-farming techniques.

He took me and Aunt Jess on a tour of the farm, showing us how they reuse and recycle materials and resources. He explained how a farm full of sheep eating grass can actually be much more eco-friendly than a farm producing corn, chickpeas, or the products that go into vegan food.

He thinks a beef burger from a small farm is more environmentally friendly than a veggie burger made in a factory.

'Factories produce pollution,' he explained. 'But they don't give anything back to the soil. Whereas cows give vital nutrients to the land with their manure. So do chickens, pigs and sheep. Plants grow in these fields. They are eaten by herbivores, who then produce manure to enrich the soil. No fossil fuels are involved. Isn't that wonderful? Isn't that the perfect system to save our planet? Imagine if someone covered these fields with concrete and built a big factory here, gushing out smoke, producing artificial foods on a conveyor belt. Would that really be better for the environment?'

I had to agree it wouldn't.

'My sheep have a good life here,' Robert said. 'They're free to roam the fields and the hillsides.'

'Until they're made into lamb chops,' I said.

Robert agreed. He said I was quite right, and dying isn't fun, whoever or whatever you are. But he also said that if you want to eat meat, then isn't it better to eat good quality animals which have led a decent life, rather than factory-farmed animals which have been tortured every day from birth to death?

'I suppose so,' I said. To be honest, by the end of our conversation, I felt quite confused. I didn't know who to believe or what to think.

But I am sure about one thing: Heathcliffe Farm is nothing like the factory farms that I've seen on films. In fact, if I was a chicken or a sheep, Heathcliffe Farm is where I would like to live.

SUNDAY 30 MARCH

I'm back home.

We stayed at the farm last night. Aunt Jess and I shared a big bed. She said, 'Kick me if I snore.' Luckily she didn't.

In the morning, we had the most enormous breakfast ever.

I didn't eat any bacon, but I did have some scrambled eggs. They were the ones that we found in the barn yesterday. Mmmm – they were delicious! I hope the hens don't mind.

Then we went for another walk around the farm with Robert, Caroline, Dotty, Viv, Ben, Pepper and George.

When it was time to say goodbye, Robert and Caroline invited me to come and stay again whenever I want.

I hope I can.

On the drive home, I couldn't stop thinking about their farm. I wish all farms could be like it. Wouldn't that be brilliant?

If we all stopped buying meat from factory farms, then factory farms wouldn't exist any more. The planet would be happier, and so would lots of animals.

We brought a surprise for Mum and Dad in the back of the car. Mum and Dad were very surprised by the surprise. In fact, they were so surprised, they wanted me and Aunt Jess to turn around, drive to the farm and give the surprise back to Robert and Caroline.

But we couldn't do that. Aunt Jess had to go home, and I can't drive, or even get the train on my own.

Plus Robert and Caroline had given the chickens to us, and it's never nice to turn down a gift.

'I thought you'd be pleased,' Aunt Jess said.

Dad couldn't believe it.

'Pleased?' he yelled. 'Are you insane? We've got a cat and a hamster and three children – isn't that enough? If you're so keen on chickens, you have them. Go on! Take them! They're all yours!'

But Aunt Jess couldn't, because she lives in a one-bedroom flat without a garden. She doesn't even have a terrace.

'They could live in your kitchen,' Dad said. 'Or the bath.'

Aunt Jess said her landlord won't let her have pets of any sort, not even a kitten, so poultry are out of the question.

In the end, Mum and Dad agreed to keep them till next weekend.

On Saturday morning, if Mum and Dad still don't like the chickens, we'll drive to Heathcliffe Farm and give them back.

'There's no "if" about it,' Dad said. 'We are not keeping these chickens.'

Actually, I think he quite likes them. He has already built them a very nice house.

MONDAY 31 MARCH

Today was the first meeting of the school council. Finn was excited all morning. He couldn't stop talking about it on the way to school. I was feeling gloomier and gloomier until Vivek came to talk to me in morning break. He said, 'Will you come with me?'

'Where?' I said.

'To the school council.'

'I can't,' I said. 'I've got maths.'

'Miss Brockenhurst says you can miss it.'

'Ha, ha.'

Vivek promised he wasn't joking. Miss Brockenhurst really had given permission for me to miss maths.

'Was it her idea?' I asked.

Vivek shook his head. 'It was mine,' he said. 'I suggested it, because I know you'll be a much better speaker than me, and you have such good ideas. So I asked Miss Brockenhurst if you could come to the school council and talk with me. She said it's up to you. Do you want to come or not?'

Obviously I did.

Finn was very surprised to see me. So was Mr Khan. He had a list of school councillors and my name wasn't anywhere to be seen. 'It's always nice to see you, Hope,' he said. 'But shouldn't you be in class now?'

'We're working together,' Vivek explained. 'She has good ideas and so do I. We want to talk about all our ideas, not just mine.'

134

Tweets	Following	Followers	Likes
1443	645	1378	922

Durdle Primary School
We love learning. This term's
values are persistence and
resilience

Tweet   Message

The first meeting of the new school council!
#democracyinaction #pupilpower #Durdleheroes

SCHOOL COUNCIL

Mr Khan looked a bit dubious, but he let me stay once he knew that Miss Brockenhurst had given me permission to miss maths.

Mr Khan asked a girl from Year 6 to go first. Then it was Finn's turn – he talked about the water park and his ideas for turning the playground into a swimming pool, then building a slide from the top of the roof. Everyone was very enthusiastic. Mr Khan promised to bring it up at the next meeting of the school governors.

When it was Vivek's turn to speak, he asked me to come with him. We walked to the front of the class together and stood side by side.

First he talked about his love of sports.

'I know we can't give up learning,' Vivek said, 'but I think we should do more sports. Also, we should have a wider range of sports at this school. What about table tennis? And hockey? And rugby? At some schools, you get a choice of sports, so different people can do different things, depending on what they're good at. But we just do football in the winter and cricket in the summer, which isn't fair if you're not any good at football or cricket.'

He got a round of applause. The rest of the school council agreed that his ideas were very sensible. Someone even described them as inspiring. Vivek couldn't stop grinning.

Then it was my turn. I described my plan for the school to go vegetarian. Luckily I could remember most of my speech from the hustings. I got a round of applause too. Everyone really liked what I said.

Vivek explained that he and his family are vegetarian, and they're all healthy, and strong too.

'He's in the school football team,' I reminded everyone.

'And the cricket team,' Vivek added.

'And he won the marathon,' I said.

'Actually,' Vivek said, 'I came second in the County Junior Quarter Marathon.'

Coming second is still amazing. So is running a quarter marathon (6.5 miles or 10.5 kilometres, which is a lot further than I could run or even walk – without complaining a lot!).

Vivek is living proof that vegetarians can be great athletes.

Mr Khan thanked us for our enthusiasm and participation. 'My ambition is to make Durdle Primary the greenest school in the country,' he said. 'With your help, I really think we can do it. Hope and Vivek, I'm very impressed by your passion and your hard work. I'm sure we can find a way of implementing some of your great ideas.'

'What about making school dinners vegetarian?' I said.

'I wish we could,' Mr Khan said. 'Unfortunately, some parents might not like it.'

'Some parents?' I was shocked. 'What about the planet? Isn't the planet more important than *some parents*?'

'I have to think about the parents,' Mr Khan said. 'They might be worried, for instance, that their children aren't getting enough protein. It's very important that the children at Durdle Primary have a balanced diet which gives them enough strength for a long school day.'

'What if we asked the parents what they think?' I said. 'What if they said yes? Would you change things?'

Mr Khan nodded. 'I don't see why not,' he said. 'But how are you going to ask all the parents? This is a big school. We have hundreds of children, which means there are almost a thousand parents and guardians. Talking to them all is a mammoth task.'

'We'll find a way,' I said.

I've been thinking about it ever since. I haven't found a solution yet. But I will.

The chickens seem to be settling in nicely. I wish we could keep them, but Dad says not a chance, our household is full enough already.

Tonight it was my turn to make tea, so I made Marcus Wilton's mum's veggie curry. He was right. It was lovely. I'm going to print out the recipe and give it to Mrs Darlington and Mrs Baptist. I hope they can make it for us all at school.

TUESDAY 1 APRIL

Today Harry gave me a meal replacement biscuit.

'This is all you need to eat all day,' he said.

'This biscuit will solve climate change,' Harry said. 'One day, the whole world will eat them. We won't need any other food.'

He told me that the biscuit was completely artificial and one hundred per cent carbon neutral. No animals were harmed during its manufacture.

I wanted to know where he had got it.

'My uncle,' he explained, 'he works in a laboratory. They're going to change the way we eat. Soon, no one will need to eat anything except these.'

The biscuit tasted just like a normal biscuit, but according to Harry, it contained all my daily nutritional requirements – including every vitamin, mineral, calorie and protein that I could possibly need.

'You won't feel hungry again till tomorrow,' Harry said.

He was wrong. At lunchtime, I was starving. But I didn't want to eat anything. I had already consumed all the vitamins, minerals, calories and proteins that I needed today.

Mrs Darlington thought I didn't like the lunch.

'I'm just not hungry,' I said.

It was too complicated to explain about the biscuit.

I was about to go to the school library, which is always open on Tuesday lunchtimes, when Harry came up to me with a big grin on his face.

'April Fool!' he said.

I can see the funny side now, but I couldn't earlier.

Harry was very apologetic.

'I thought you'd laugh,' he said. 'I was just joking. I didn't mean to make you feel stupid. I'm very sorry.'

He asked if there was anything he could do to make me feel better.

'You could come up with one of your brilliant ideas,' I said.

I told him about Mr Khan and the school council and asking all the parents and carers what they think about vegetarian lunches.

Harry went away to have a good think and came back later with an idea. It's a good one, a really good one. I can't tell you about it yet, because it's got to be a surprise. But if you read my blog tomorrow, you'll find out everything.

I've been learning about the food that chickens like. We bought a bag of chicken food, but they can have lots of treats too, mostly our leftovers. Apparently chickens love potato skins and cooked rice. They're also keen on fruit and veg, although you have to chop it first, so they don't choke.

Mr Crabbe came round to complain about the noise.

Actually, he didn't exactly come round, he just poked his head over the fence.

He stared at the chickens for a long time. Then he said, 'What are they?'

'Chickens,' I said.

'I can see that. What are they doing here?'

'They've come to live with us.'

He said, 'I hope this is an April Fool because I'm not putting up with that terrible racket all night long.'

'You don't have to worry,' I said. 'They're asleep at night, just like us, so they don't make any noise.'

'They'd better not,' Mr Crabbe said, 'otherwise I'll be calling the council. Have you got a licence for keeping wildlife in your garden?'

'You don't need a licence for chickens,' I said.

Luckily Mum had already looked it up on the council's website, so I knew what I was talking about.

Mr Crabbe is not the only one who doesn't like the chickens. Poppadom hates them too. I think she's actually terrified of them, which is quite strange because she's not usually scared of birds. I still haven't recovered from the time that she brought a dead sparrow into my bedroom and left it on my pillow.

I suppose chickens are quite a lot bigger than sparrows, and make more noise. Poppadom won't go anywhere near them. She doesn't even like going in the garden any more. She just sits by the window, staring at the chickens.

Hope Jones' Blog

WEDNESDAY 2 APRIL

It's amazing how much you can achieve if you're determined, and you have good friends who are willing to help.

Harry is a genius, even if he says so himself. I can't wait to see his ideas which will save the planet – they are going to transform human existence. I'm completely confident about that. Maybe he really will invent a biscuit which contains all our daily nutritional requirements and is entirely carbon neutral.

His latest idea hasn't transformed human existence, but it is going to make a big difference to Durdle Primary. I'm confident about that too.

Finn and I asked Mum to take us to school fifteen minutes early. She said it made a nice change from having to shout at us to get us out of the house on time.

We weren't the first to arrive, Harry had got there before us. Vivek arrived a minute later. We were all in our positions ten minutes before the gates opened. We came prepared. We each had a clipboard, a piece of lined paper and a pencil.

Harry had brought some chalk and wrote on the pavement outside the school so everyone crossing the road would know what we were doing.

Everyone arrived in a rush. Suddenly the street was full of people bringing children to the school. The four of us couldn't possibly talk to all of them, but we did our best.

'Excuse me?' I said again and again. 'Would you like to read our petition? Will you take a copy of this letter? Do you care about the planet?'

Most parents hurried their children straight past us without even stopping to look or listen, let alone say, 'Good morning.'

Mum told me not to be offended. She said the mums and dads

are often in a panic in the mornings, because they need to drop their kids off, then get to work on time.

Some of the children and parents did stop to talk to us. They wanted to know what we were doing. Several signed the petition, others took the letter, a few even promised to write an email to Mr Khan.

We stayed till the bell rang.

All day different people came up to me and asked about the petition. They wanted to know what we were doing and why.

Some of them said it sounded stupid, others said they would never give up eating meat, but the majority were very positive. They said they cared about the planet and they would be happy to have vegetarian lunches – as long as they could carry on eating burgers and fish fingers for tea.

At the end of the day, all four of us rushed back to the school entrance, and asked more people to sign the petition.

Harry had printed out fifty letters. This morning, we handed out thirty-three. This afternoon, we gave out the remaining seventeen. Harry is going to print another fifty tonight and bring them to school tomorrow. We all agreed to arrive fifteen minutes early again. We're going to carry on doing the petition until we've got a hundred signatures, then we'll present it to Mr Khan. He'll have to listen to us! He can't ignore a hundred people, can he?

Wednesday 2 April

Dear Parents and Carers of children at Durdle Primary

My name is Hope Jones, I am ten years old, and I want to live on this planet for the next sixty or seventy years. Maybe even a hundred! I want to share the planet with your children, and all the other kids around the world who are growing up now.

But there is a problem.

The atmosphere is getting hotter. The oceans are rising. Weather is changing. Soon parts of our planet will become uninhabitable – unless we take action quickly!

One of the major causes of climate change is factory farming and meat production. So I am suggesting our school makes one small change. Instead of having meat for every school lunch, we could all have vegetarian lunches three times a week on Mondays, Tuesdays and Thursdays.

I know some people think it's important for children to eat meat, which is why I am not suggesting the school goes completely vegetarian.

Being vegetarian three days a week would be easy, and would make a difference.

I hope you agree this is a good idea. If you do, please sign our petition, and tell Mr Khan.

Thank you!
Hope Jones
(Otters class)

THURSDAY 3 APRIL

This morning, Harry, Vivek, Finn and I did the petition again.

Lots more people wanted to sign!

We were surrounded by a big crowd when Mr Khan came out and asked us to stop.

He said we weren't allowed to make political statements on school property.

'This isn't school property,' I said. 'This is the pavement, it's public, anyone is allowed to stand here.'

Mr Khan had to admit I was right.

I asked if he would like to sign the petition himself.

'No, thank you. I don't think that would be appropriate.'

Apparently teachers aren't allowed to get involved in politics.

Even so, he stood there till the bell rang, watching us and saying good morning to parents and kids.

At lunchtime, I showed the petition and the letter to Mrs Darlington and Mrs Baptist. They both said they couldn't sign it.

'That wouldn't be right,' Mrs Darlington said. 'This is for the parents, not us.'

'What do you think about my idea?' I asked. 'Would you be happy to cook vegetarian food for everyone?'

'We wouldn't mind,' Mrs Baptist said.

'Your book has given us lots of good ideas,' Mrs Darlington said. 'The other night, I made the chickpea fritters for my son's tea. He loved them.'

'I love them too!' I told her that I've been cooking for my family every Monday. She was very impressed.

I did the petition again after school.

This time, it was just me. Vivek and Finn both had football, and Harry had coding club, but I didn't mind being alone. I like chatting to people, everyone was very friendly. Even Miss Brockenhurst gave me a thumbs-up.

I got another seventeen signatures and handed out the rest of the letters.

We've already got more than a hundred signatures on the petition, but we don't want to stop yet.

We'll be back tomorrow!

Tonight Sparkle and Tariq came round to meet the chickens. They'd heard all about our new pets from Becca.

I feel like I'm getting to know the chickens – they each have a different character. One of them is shy and nervous, another is very confident, the third is quite affectionate and always comes to say hello.

'You should give them names,' Sparkle said.

I would like to give them names, but I can't, not yet, because I'd be even more upset if we had to give them back. For now, they're just the three chickens.

Sparkle said, 'I hope you're not going to eat them.'

'Of course not!' I told her. That would be like eating Poppadom or Chutney. I would never eat my pets!

'What about their eggs?' Sparkle asked.

'We probably will eat the eggs,' I admitted.

The chickens aren't contributing to climate change, they're just eating our scraps. And they have a happy life here in our garden, living in the lovely house that Dad built for them.

Sparkle tried to persuade me that I should be a vegan, not a flexitarian, but I can't see anything wrong with eating the odd egg.

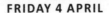
FRIDAY 4 APRIL

The petition was even more successful today. It has now been signed by two hundred and sixty-three people.

Finn and I were the first to arrive in the morning. Harry came next with his mum, then Vivek with his dad. The parents all chatted to one another while the four of us got ready with our petitions and our letters.

We handed out another fifty letters. At least twenty parents promised to email Mr Khan over the weekend.

There was a Year 1 bake sale after school, so we got lots more signatures. And Harry's mum bought us each a cupcake, which was very nice of her. They were baked by Gwen's mum, who promised they were nut-free and vegetarian, but not vegan, because they contained some butter, milk and eggs.

'I'll have yours if you don't want it,' Finn said.

Ordinarily I might have given it to him, but I thought I should treat myself on a Friday afternoon. That's what being a flexitarian is all about.

We were just thinking about leaving when Mr Khan came out of the main entrance and marched up to us.

I said, 'Good afternoon, Mr Khan. Would you like to sign our petition today?'

'It's time to stop your protest,' Mr Khan said.

I started to argue, but he interrupted me.

'Don't worry,' he said, 'it's all going to be fine.'

'No, it's not!' I told him. 'The planet is in trouble, we're in a climate emergency. Nothing is going to be fine!'

'I don't know about the planet,' Mr Khan said. 'But your protest has been a success – we're going to change the menus.'

I couldn't believe it. We'd won!

Mr Khan said, 'I've been very impressed by your courage, energy and perseverance. I'm also impressed by your team spirit and co-operation. You've done something amazing, Hope. I'm proud of you. Have a lovely weekend. When you come to school on Monday, I'll tell you all about the changes that we're going to make.'

I can't wait!

'Congratulations! This is great news,' said Harry's mum to us four. 'Let's celebrate. How about another cupcake?'

Hope Jones' Blog

SATURDAY 5 APRIL

We are keeping the chickens!

Today was meant to be their final day. Aunt Jess rang up to ask if she had to take them back to Robert's farm.

Dad said, 'We don't mind them, we'll keep them for now.'

Actually, he loves them. We all do – it's like they're part of the family.

Now we need to think of names for them. Dad suggested Scrambled, Poached and Fried, which wasn't very nice. Mum said how about Faith, Hope and Charity, which is nicer, but not very exciting.

Finn wants to name them after Marcus Wilton and two more Manchester United strikers. I like Marcus Wilton – I'm not interested in football, but if I was, he would be my favourite player – but even so I don't think any of the chickens should be named after him.

Becca had the best idea. She thought we should name them after her three favourite female artists, who are Frida Kahlo, Cornelia Parker and Leonora Carrington. She showed me some of their pictures and I absolutely loved them, but 'Frida, Cornelia and Leonora' is a bit of a mouthful.

We're all going to have a serious think tomorrow. Do you have a brilliant idea? If so, let me know ASAP.

SUNDAY 6 APRIL

Thank you for emailing me so many brilliant ideas for the chickens' names! I have just spent ages going through all your messages — there are some great ones.

I liked the Good, the Bad and the Ugly. Thank you for that suggestion, Sergio.

Thank you, Dylan, for suggesting the Three Wise Men (Caspar, Melchior and Balthasar). There's just one problem: these chickens are girls.

I loved the idea of calling them after Greek goddesses. Thank you, Mary, for suggesting Athena, Artemis and Aphrodite. Unfortunately, these chickens don't look very Greek. Or much like goddesses.

In the end, I thought the simplest was the best. The chickens are now called Henny, Penny and Jenny. Thank you to Rita, who suggested those names. If you would like a gift of six eggs, please send me your address.

On second thoughts, Rita, you might have to come and collect your prize yourself, because I don't think I could send eggs in the post. I'll send you my address. But don't come over immediately. The chickens haven't actually laid any eggs yet, so we don't even have one, let alone half a dozen.

Henny   Penny   Jenny

Today Granny and Grandad came to meet the chickens. It was the first really nice warm sunny day of the year, so we had a barbecue to celebrate.

The barbecue was brilliant. Mitch offered to bring burgers, sausages and chicken legs for the omnivores, but I asked him not to.

'The meat will be free range,' Mitch promised, 'and organic.'

'Maybe next time,' I said.

This time, I wanted the barbie to be entirely meat-free. We had cauliflower steaks, courgette kebabs, veggie burgers, halloumi cheese, portobello mushrooms and corn on the cob. It was all delicious. And I've learned something new today: I thought I hated courgettes, because they've always been disgusting, but they're actually very tasty when they're grilled on our barbecue.

Even Mitch thought lunch was scrumptious, and he is a committed carnivore.

'I'd better watch out,' he said, 'you'll be turning me vegan soon. That would be bad for business.'

I was really worried when I saw him talking to Sparkle. I thought they must be having an argument. But actually they were discussing their favourite Scottish islands.

I never knew they both loved kayaking.

You know what? Mitch and Sparkle had never actually talked properly before. They had only glared at one another through the shop window while Mitch was working inside and Sparkle was protesting outside. It turns out they get on quite well.

Grandad didn't tease me once. He even ate a cauliflower steak! I don't think he liked it very much, because he only took a couple of bites, but at least he tried. He did make a joke

Henny

Penny

Jenny

about eating the chickens, but he apologised straight away, and promised never to say anything horrible about them again. Which is good, because they really are members of our family now.

Only one person didn't like the barbecue. You can probably guess who that was.

But even he cheered up when I offered him a veggie burger.

MONDAY 7 APRIL

This morning, in assembly, Mr Khan made an announcement to the whole school.

He said, 'Did you enjoy the sunshine at the weekend? I didn't. Because I was inside, reading over one hundred emails that I had received from parents and carers over the past few days.'

He said his inbox had literally exploded.

He said every message except one was extremely positive. He didn't tell us what the one negative message said, but I think it must have been quite rude, because I saw Miss Brockenhurst and Miss Candover giving one another a look.

Anyway, Mr Khan has been convinced by the enthusiastic response from pupils, staff and parents. Starting tomorrow, school dinners will be entirely vegetarian at least three times a week.

He asked me, Vivek, Harry and Finn to come up to the front. The whole school gave us a round of applause. It was quite embarrassing, I blushed a lot, but I also felt very proud. We did it! We won.

Mr Khan shook my hand.

'You are a very impressive young woman,' he said. 'What are you going to change next?'

'The world,' I said.

After lunch, I had a long chat with Mrs Darlington and Mrs Baptist.

They're not worried about cooking vegetarian food on Mondays, Tuesdays and Thursdays. Actually, they're both looking forward to the new menu. They think it will be fun.

They've got lots of good ideas already. To start with, they are going to try something simple for lunch tomorrow: veggie lasagna with carrots and beans. But they are already planning more adventurous options for next term. They're going to make filo pastry parcels with a feta cheese and broad bean filling; spicy rice with fiery chilli sauce; homemade veggie sausages, served with mashed potato; and Marcus Wilton's mum's veggie curry.

Mrs Darlington and Mrs Baptist think I should go into politics. They said they would both vote for me as Prime Minister. Unfortunately I'm too young, because you have to be eighteen to stand for parliament.

'You should do it anyway,' Mrs Baptist said, 'you'd still be better than those idiots running the country at the moment.'

'She couldn't be any worse,' added Mrs Darlington.

TUESDAY 8 APRIL

Today was the first all-vegetarian menu at school. It was delicious. I'm not just saying that, it really was, everyone said so.

The lunch wasn't vegan. The lasagna contained milk and cheese, and the custard was made of eggs and milk.

But like Mr Khan said: 'Nobody's perfect.'

DURDLE PRIMARY
:-) Lunch Menu :-)
Tuesday 8th April

MAIN
Vegetarian Lasagna

VEGETABLES
Chopped carrots, green beans

DESSERT
Pineapple upside-down cake
with custard

EXTRAS
Freshly baked bread, fresh fruit,
yoghurt, drinking water

Durdle Primary is a healthy living school.
We hope our children will always eat at least
5 portions of fruit and veg every day.

Next term, we're going to plant a herb garden in the playground, so our school dinners can have more fresh herbs. We might grow some fruit and vegetables too.

Maybe one day we really will be the greenest school in the country.

Tweets	Following	Followers	Likes
1458	649	1385	933

Durdle Primary School
We love learning. This term's values are persistence and resilience

Tweet   Message

Our first vegetarian lunch for the whole school! Yum! Can I have seconds, please? #MeatFreeMonday #Durdlehero

Hope Jones' Blog

THURSDAY 10 APRIL

Hello, Marcus!

I know you've been reading my blog, because you sent me such a great photo.

Thank you!

I've given it to Mrs Darlington and Mrs Baptist already. They were absolutely delighted. They've pinned it on the wall of their kitchen.

They are your biggest fans – apart from Finn, obviously.

And me now too!

Today they cooked your mum's veggie curry for the whole school – everyone said it was delicious.

SATURDAY 12 APRIL

You're never going to believe what happened today – Jenny laid an egg.

It might not have been Jenny. Henny or Penny could have laid it just as easily. I wasn't actually there to see what happened. But I think the egg is Jenny's, because she was the only chicken who got cross when I picked it up.

If this egg is yours, Jenny, I'm very sorry. I feel bad about taking it away. But at least you have a nice life in our garden, don't you?

I wanted to keep the egg till we had at least five, but Mum wanted to cook it straight away. 'I've never eaten an egg this fresh,' she said.

I haven't forgotten the six eggs that I promised to Rita. (Hello, Rita!) But we're going to try them first.

We did wait till Becca got up. She went to another party with Tariq last night, so she didn't come downstairs for ages.

She said, 'You shouldn't have waited for me. I'm not even hungry.'

'That's lucky,' I said. 'We're only going to have one fifth of an egg each.'

I fried the egg myself, with Mum watching to make sure I didn't burn the house down.

Robert was right – fresh eggs do taste better. Especially if you collected them from your own garden.

Sparkle, if you're reading this, I'm sorry, I know you'll be disappointed in me. I'm not a very good vegan.

Mum says I shouldn't worry so much because I've cut down on my meat intake and so has she, not to mention the rest of our family.

Nobody's perfect – but at least we're making a difference.

Thanks for reading my blog. I hope you want to save the world too. Here are ten ways that you can help. Good luck! Love from Hope.

1. Maybe you don't want to be a vegan or a vegetarian, but it's easy to be a flexitarian. Why don't you try? You could only eat meat once a day, for instance. Or every other day. Or just at the weekends.

2. Try to find out where your food came from. Look on the label. Ask questions. Talk to the owners or the managers of your local shops and supermarkets. Ask if they stock organic and free-range meat, cheese, milk and eggs. You'll find out that factory-farmed meat and dairy is much cheaper than organic and free-range, but it's cheap for a reason.

3. Cook a meal. You could try lentil soup. It's easy – and very tasty! Obviously ask your parents first and don't use a stove or sharp knives without an adult nearby.

4. Obviously you can't vote for me to be on the school council. I wish you could! But do you have a school council at your school? Why don't you stand to be a school councillor? Or you could talk to the school councillors and ask their opinions about food, school dinners, factory farming and flexitarians.

5. Have you read *Charlotte's Web*? If not, why not?

6. Visit a farm. Talk to a farmer. I know it's not easy for everyone. Maybe you live miles from the nearest farm. But you could try to visit one at the weekend or on holiday.

7. If you can't get to a farm, you could visit a farm shop instead. Or a farmers' market. You can usually meet the farmers who grew the food, chat to them and ask lots of questions. And you can buy really fresh food – which has come straight from the farm to you.

8. Read a book, watch a movie, search on the internet – and find out more about farming, food and climate change. Just one thing: don't watch any movies about factory farms, because they're so disgusting.

9. Plant some seeds. It's easy. You can just buy a packet of seeds and plant them in some little pots. Cress, parsley, lettuce, tomatoes and beans will all grow quickly and be delicious to eat. If you've got a garden, you can plant even more. Or you could get some chickens! They're so nice! And their eggs are very tasty.

10. Go outside. Go for a walk. Look at the trees. Climb a hill. Our planet is beautiful. Remember why we care about it. Remember what we are fighting for.